LOVE AND WAR WESTERN STYLE

ROSE SCOLLARD

Brave & Brilliant Series
ISSN 2371-7238 (Print) ISSN 2371-7246 (Online)

University of Calgary Press
2500 University Drive NW
Calgary, Alberta
Canada T2N 1N4
press.ucalgary.ca

LIBRARY AND ARCHIVES CANADA CATALOGUING IN PUBLICATION

Title: Love and war western style / Rose Scollard.
Other titles: Love and war western style (Compilation)
Names: Scollard, Rose, author. | Container of (work): Scollard, Rose. Don't fence me in. | Container of (work): Scollard, Rose. Pretzel maker. | Container of (work): Scollard, Rose. Love and war western style.
Series: Brave & brilliant series ; no. 42.
Description: Series statement: Brave & brilliant series, 2371-7238 ; no. 42
Identifiers: Canadiana (print) 20250108933 | Canadiana (ebook) 20250108941 | ISBN 9781773856148 (hardcover) | ISBN 9781773856155 (softcover) | ISBN 9781773856162 (PDF) | ISBN 9781773856179 (EPUB)
Subjects: LCGFT: Drama.
Classification: LCC PS8587.C615 L68 2025 | DDC C812/.54—dc23

The University of Calgary Press acknowledges the support of the Government of Alberta through the Alberta Media Fund for our publications. We acknowledge the financial support of the Government of Canada. We acknowledge the financial support of the Canada Council for the Arts for our publishing program.

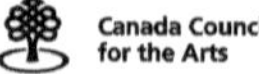

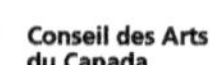

Editing by Aritha van Herk
Copy editing by Andrew Goodwin
Cover image: Colourbox 4569214
Cover design, page design, and typesetting by Melina Cusano

For Elizabeth and Peter
and those treasured radio days.

CONTENTS

Crickets or
How I Read a Radio Play
Kathleen Flaherty
IX

INTRODUCTION
1

PLAYS
Don't Fence Me In
13
The Pretzel Maker
39
Love and War Western Style
63

CRICKETS OR
HOW TO READ A RADIO PLAY

The minute I revisit a script of Rose Scollard's, I am reminded of how effortlessly Rose refers to "old timey" radio plays at the same time as using them to comic effect and commentary on contemporary Alberta. She fulfills all the demands of radio for clear context, recognizable voices, evocative sound effects and music that grabs listeners by the ears and keeps them listening.

All good radio plays speak to our ears, locate us aurally, starting with the first sound cue, music cue or line of dialogue. Because there is no re-wind button on the airwaves, the radio audience is in complete control. If they don't "get it" in the first minute or so, or they don't like what they hear, they can change the station, leave the room, turn it off. They need to know who, what, where, when in very quick order.

How you make that happen usually starts with music and sound. An upright piano tinkling ragtime evokes an era. When you add the sounds of glasses hitting a bar, maybe a split door swinging and male laughter, you are in a saloon in the Old West. These are stereotypes, clichés, tropes that are easily identified by a large portion of the audience that a radio signal reaches. And, although times have changed and cultural audioscapes have multiplied and fragmented, many of those clichés still do the same work they did in the 1940s. The more you lean on those stereotypes now, the more likely they are to signal that you are intending the audience to read some form of comedy. So, within ten seconds of hearing the first music and sound, you have an idea of where and when. Then, with a bit of dialogue, you either reinforce or update that impression.

Let's take Rose's play *Don't Fence Me In*:

TWANGY WESTERN VOICE SINGS "DON'T FENCE ME IN." APPROACHING HOOFBEATS.

GENERAL HUBBUB, FOLKS TALKING EXCITEDLY, "IT'S MITCH CARTER."

"KINCAID BETTER WATCH OUT." "MITCH'LL FIX 'IM."

One music cue and two sound cues, you think, Old West, gunslinger, and shoot-outs in the street. Somebody named Mitch is set up to be a main character. The dialogue you hear next reinforces that impression: voices speak "classic Western" lines that add details, indicate that Mitch is some kind of hero. What the listener doesn't see, the cues to the radio producer and the actors, like the character names "Bad Guy One" and "Shady Lady," suggest that we are in the territory of caricature, maybe even parody.

If the next thing you heard was a line like, "Cut. Reset for the top of the scene," followed by someone talking movie biz talk, you would re-set immediately and know you are on a movie set although you don't know yet when or who. In the case of *Don't Fence Me In*, you learn that you are in unexpected territory when you are introduced to the horse, who lets you know he's imaginary. "Maybe it's not the Old West," you think, "maybe . . . ?" Your mind assimilates this new information you are ready to re-imagine, to follow the cues to find out what's going on. When we make a radio play, we are careful to set and re-set with music and sound and voices to keep the listening ear in the experience with a minimum of confusion. When a listener gets confused for more than a few seconds, when they stop listening and start wondering, they lose the thread and have to rewind to catch up, which was not possible in the time before streaming. You've lost them. Sometimes engaging dialogue is enough to keep the mind in the flow; sometimes interesting music and intricate abstract sound are enough to propel the audio experience; there are no absolute rules. But in the context of network radio, when there were audiences in the thousands across the country listening in real time, we had to create work that would speak to a large and diverse population of individuals, who were most likely doing something else at the same time—making lunch, doing dishes, yard work, housework, exercising, driving a car. It had to be broad enough and bold enough to retain comprehension and engagement.

So, of course, sound effects and ambiences need to quickly set place and mood. They need to be general enough to be easily recognizable to most people—a café, a laundromat, a hockey rink, a school hallway, a rodeo, a rock concert, a campfire by night. You heard those in your head, right?

By some twist of fate, night scenes can be set with one sound: crickets. It doesn't matter that there are no crickets in many places in North America at night. We all get it: crickets mean it's night. Add a crackling fire and you've got a range of possible night scenes. Bring in a soft guitar and you've got something cozy and benign. If there's a dark drone underneath with long flute sounds or an off tune piano, well, that's another story. It's all in our heads. In fact, some of these sounds are just what we imagine something sounds like, not actually what something sounds like. Sounds, especially ambiences, have to be generic enough to be recognizable as a certain class of settings—a city, a meadow, a large body of water. At the same time, most sounds also need to be specific enough to give us information about this particular place and time: What season is it? Is the rain soft or hard? Wet snow? Dry snow? Beware of ambience that comes from a truly wrong location. Some of the most irritated listeners who wrote us at the CBC about location errors were from the legion of birders in Canada, who couldn't enjoy a play that had the wrong birds in it.

Still, there are places where audio can go, from jungles to outer space, that would be very difficult to afford in a film or on television. Most of us have aural templates for those places, so the opening line of dialogue doesn't have to be, "Well, here we are in an airplane."

Spot effects, or action effects, are those sounds that indicate what is happening right in the moment. They were sometimes created by the actors themselves, who picked up paper, sipped from glasses, undid zippers, and walked on wood or gravel or sand on small surfaces available in the studio. Picture three or four actors standing around a microphone, each rhythmically squeezing a box of cornstarch, "walking" on a snowy Alberta night. Or an actor lifting her head in and out of a big bowl of water as she swims for Olympic gold.

The more elaborate effects, as well as those that could be added afterward or had to occur simultaneously with the dialogue, were provided by the sound effects technicians, those geniuses who created sounds from scratch. I'll never forget the sight of Eric Wagers in a live radio play we did at the Edmonton Fringe creating a fight scene with the cast. The actors provided the skin-on-skin sounds as well as the *Ughs* and *Oofs*, while Eric tore up celery and bashed watermelons to create limb tearing and head punches. The audience screamed with delight.

Sometimes a sound we expected would be easy to find in the library of recorded effects proved most elusive. Like the bell that rings when you open the door of one of those old-fashioned cafes. We needed that for Thomas King's series, *The Dead Dog Café Comedy Hour* and eventually built it ourselves and attached it to the studio door to ring whenever we opened it. The door, by the way, was a fixture of most radio drama studios. It usually weighed in at a couple of hundred pounds and had two or three different doors and two or three different windows set within, each made of different material.

Ambiences and sound effects weren't our only tools; we also used music to create mood, atmosphere and location. In one series, *The Seven Dudley Sins*, written by former Saskatchewan writer Greg Nelson and set in a fictional small Alberta town, many episodes began with a few bars of Brian Tate's theme music crossing into an obviously small-town church congregation singing a traditional hymn. This hymn receded and faded into another ambience behind the voice of the central character, the new minister, Kevin. The ambience would then unfold full blown into a scene in the coffee shop or the manse or wherever it happened to be. The music, which was used for the opening theme, closing credits, and transitions, was heavily flavoured with the major chord progressions of classic hymns from hymn books favoured by the United Church, and featured an organ much of the orchestration. I had over a dozen different hymn books in my office, and Brian and I had a great time making selections and trying to teach them to the cast. He would record the melody so they could hear it when they sang. We would move six or seven people around to various spots in the studio and for each take ask them to sing to the music in their headphones as different characters, then lay the takes on top of each other and match the music underneath. Some days the choir was better than other days.

The musical scene transitions could either be longer, say ten seconds, or shorter, four to six seconds, phrases that led from one scene to the next, picking up the tone of the scene and offering a way to hear the next scene. Or, the music might be a "sting," a bit of hard punctuation to the scene's ending—an emphatic period, a question, a comic comment—followed by a few seconds of silence and the ambience of the next scene. Brian created a bank of these for the eventually twenty-six half hours of the *Dudley* series, which was augmented by special cues for each episode.

We at the CBC were lucky to be able to commission composers for many of the radio plays and series we produced. We also had a blanket user license that paid royalties to composers and musicians for whatever music already existing that we had access to, millions of pieces of music of all genres, styles, and moods. Of course, we had Canadian content regulations that were intricate but essentially insisted on fifty per cent or more Canadian music. I won't get into the arcane world of what defines Canadian content because it's not as Canadian as you might think. Suffice it to say that, along with the joy of deciding what music was appropriate for the play you were working on, you had to figure out the CanCon rules, and each little bit of music had to be logged onto a network database that went to SOCAN, which distributed the royalties.

Choosing music was one of my favourite parts of the job—I imagined I was good at it—and the choices started with a discussion about whatever music the writer envisioned for the scene. In my work, the scenes themselves were rarely underscored, unless the genre or period seemed to demand it. I prefer to let the nuance of the dialogue tell the story, allowing the listener to decide how to feel about it. Because music is potent.

As is the human voice. I don't want to credit the wrong person with saying this, but early in my radio learning I was offered a piece of wisdom that meant a great deal to me: "The voice creates its own context." To me that encapsulated how, when we hear a voice, we know something about the person talking outside of what they are saying. Accents are obvious indications of place of origin and, in some contexts, social class. I am not knowledgeable enough about accents from places other than North America to be able to discern many of the nuances of social class, so the only way I could be sure I got it right was to cast someone who had the accent we needed. There were a few older actors who could do all kinds of accents very convincingly. For the most part, though, I preferred to find actors who actually spoke with those accents, which sometimes led me quite far afield to working with actors I had never met or seen.

But accents are only a tiny bit of it. High voices, low, warm voices, cool. Many voices have interesting textures based on the physiology of the person and their breathing. Some voices are clear and clean. Some people have crisp diction, others less so. Some people sound too contemporary and out of place in period drama. Mom voices, bad biker voices, announcer voices, urban voices, young, old, white, black, Indigenous, educated, mysterious. And often misleading. Without visuals, when I wanted the listener to picture a big dangerous guy, I found an actor with a deep voice. Never mind that most guys, even big guys, have tenor voices—a deep voice makes it easier to picture a big villain.

But, of course, they can't all have deep voices. Everyone in a drama must sound different, so that they don't have to call each other by name all the time. You may have noticed that people in radio dramas do quite a bit of addressing each other by name, especially at the beginning. Some writers and actors make this unnatural quirk sound perfectly normal, but it does get tedious in big scenes, so identifiably differentiated voices are necessary. Even a seasoned producer can make the mistake of casting someone for how they look, forgetting that how they sound is what allows the listener to conjure their looks for themselves. Once you've accidentally cast two actors who sound alike because you've forgotten what they really sound like, you aren't likely to make that mistake again. In fact, I eventually made a practice of auditioning people over the phone so I wouldn't be swayed by their looks into casting them for a movie of the mind.

But back to Rose's horse, Boss, "short for Boscoe." How does he sound? Before the ubiquity of CGI, radio was the only medium besides animation to allow writers the opportunity to fill real and imaginary worlds with imaginary creatures. When I picture Rose's horse, he is a cartoon, and, not surprisingly, his whole world begins to look like a cartoon in my head. That undoubtedly affects the way I cast the play and how I direct the actors, in the hopes that you'll see what I see, you'll "get" what I "get" from the script. What you actually imagine or see in your mind's eye I will never know, but it doesn't really matter as long as we are sharing the story, the jokes, and the emotions as they've been written. Boss, the imaginary horse, is actually the narrator of the play. The narrator, a common feature of audio plays, helps to paint the pictures, fill in the blanks and move from one place or time to another, leaving room for the dialogue to create character and develop the action of the play.

A big challenge for radio writers and actors is the scale of performance. Yes, there are thousands of listeners. At the same time, you are talking to one person wearing headphones, jogging in the park, or relaxing in bed at night with the lights off. Characters can speak quietly, intimately, to each other or in their heads and the microphone will catch it so it's loud enough to hear. On the other hand, there is little need to project the voice except when calling from one room to another or out on a baseball diamond. And as for yelling/screaming in anger, a little goes a long way. Mics don't tolerate a lot of loud sounds directly into their diaphragms, so actors had to learn not to blow air directly into the mic (popping) or to push the sound into distortion. In truth, anger is only rarely expressed by yelling.

The intimacy of audio also encourages a raw honesty of performance. Every emotion changes breathing and alters vocal quality, so actors have to believe in what they are saying. Physical action also affects breathing and vocal quality, so the studio could be full of actors swinging imaginary axes as they chopped wood, mimicking or actually doing physical activity. As well, they activated emotion that resembled silent film acting to make sure that emotion was evident.

CBC Radio Drama was discontinued in 2012, although budgets had been shrinking for some time before that. Appointment listening was being replaced by streamed audio, audio on demand. Podcasts became the way people listened to audio fiction or non-fiction.

Oddly, the pandemic brought about a resurgence of interest in making and consuming what we used to call radio drama and is now called audio drama. The means of production are readily available and the internet means you can reach people all over the world. This creates both challenge and opportunity for the makers because the many cultures of the world do not necessarily share the same sound references or social cues that make it possible for us to understand the settings, characters, or even the tone of a narrative. It's hard to know whether this allows for niche audiences—for more diverse, eclectic and experimental work—or if it just encourages global monoculture. Probably both.

I bet we all still understand crickets, though.

And it is evident how skilled Rose Scollard is as a radio writer. In the first two pages of a script, less than a minute, she has plopped us into a place and the beginnings of an intriguing story. And we are hooked. What happens next?

Kathleen Flaherty
May 2024

INTRODUCTION

I've had a lot of fun in my writing life, but absolutely the most fun was in the late eighties and early nineties creating radio plays for the CBC in Calgary.

First of all, I was paid—something I had not experienced much as a playwright. Second, the actual writing was immensely pleasurable. I seemed to tap into a different dimension than when I was writing for the stage. Voices and sound effects popped up spontaneously. I was transported back into the radio world I had experienced as a child, and ideas and conversations came to me instinctively and unconstrained. Even the editing was fun. My reader/advisor, often another playwright, would pile on suggestion after suggestion, leaving me with the challenge of incorporating reams of proposed additions without going over the rigidly enforced time allotment. Paring down what I had written to include new dialogue and ideas was an intriguing puzzle, and never a chore.

Then there was the production. I would turn up at the CBC building on Westmount Boulevard in Calgary, now just an empty lot, alas. There, I would be met by the Director, Martie Fishman who, once he had waved me through security, would lead me down a narrow hall to the tiny control room already crammed with actors and technicians. There was always a buzz of excitement and goodwill in that room. There were limits on time, but no restrictions at all on the number of actors, so there might be a dozen or more people waiting to bring my half-hour drama to life. Introductions would be made and then, with sound engineer Bob Doble and sound effects technician Ute Schaffland at the console, Martie would begin. Radio actors were not required to memorize their lines, and so the rehearsal process was ultra simple. Working scene by scene, Martie would run the actors through the script once, rarely twice, then take them into the studio and begin recording, with Bob operating the console and he and Ute, always so creative, adding sound effects. I remember one occasion when the sound of pigeons flapping in an abandoned house was needed and Bob, unhappy with the pigeon recordings available to him, created the flapping sound himself, with two huge leather mittens.

And I still have in my head an image of Ute at the live broadcast of *The Pretzel Maker* clopping the proverbial coconuts together for the hero's romantic entrance on a horse.

Often, more than simple effects were needed. Many scenes called for specific background sound. While some plays didn't need added sound at all—*The Pretzel Maker*, for instance, was set in a tea dance at the Palliser Hotel and was broadcast live from the midst of an actual tea dance that provided the ambience—most recorded dramas had complicated audio requirements. "PILLAGE, GUNFIRE, MAYHEM, CRIES OF ANGUISH!" and "DOOR OF SALOON PUSHED OPEN—DEN OF SIN SOUNDS" in *Don't Fence Me In*, were typical examples, as was my favourite, "TOWN BEING TORN UP, PAINTED RED, AND SENT TO THE DEVIL." Such sound cues required more than single effects, and usually the whole group was called into service, including the playwright. At Martie's direction, we would cram into the recording room and shout or weep or groan or gasp according to what was needed, until we achieved an acceptable atmosphere for the scene.

It would take only a couple of hours to record the play, then the next day I would go back to hear the soundtrack being added. This was the most marvelous aspect to me, that a composer and performers would be hired to create music for the play. A few more sound effects might be added at that time.

Unless you were born before 1950 in North America or Europe, you won't have had much experience of the unique nature of radio drama. Sound is a sensory medium that is not limited to the strictly auditory. It is also a medium that can convey more than words, creating not only visual and aural landscapes but emotional milieus as well. "I live right inside radio when I listen." This quote, often attributed to Marshall McLuhan but in fact gleaned by him from a participant in a radio poll, deftly sums up the experience of listening to radio. McLuhan saw radio as a "tribal drum" that pulled listeners into an archetypal and communal fold, and indeed radio drama has often been compared to the ancient practice of storytelling where listeners crowded around a fire to hear ghost stories, hero sagas and comic tales. The storyteller, having them in thrall, relied on them to bring their own imaginations into play to re-create the story visually and emotionally as it was being told. Radio drama, like storytelling, demands imaginative cooperation from the audience, inducing the listeners to create in their minds the world being presented. The effect is deeply involving and satisfying.

It seemed to me all those years ago that what I was listening to on the radio was literally inside my head. I was an avid reader as a child, disappearing completely into whatever book I was reading. But radio was a different kind of immersion. It had a way of resonating that called up subconscious participation in the listener. Reading, no matter how far I fell down the rabbit hole, was cerebral. My response to radio, on the other hand, was intuitive, almost feral. The voices and sounds I heard called up vivid pictures in my mind, as though I were collaborating with the sound, imaginatively building the world as it was being enacted.

Because listeners are more vulnerable to sound than to graphic imagery, and more easily captivated and manipulated, radio is a perfect medium for horror stories. I've rarely felt as much revulsion or fear reading ghost stories or watching horror films as I did listening to such shows as *Inner Sanctum* or *Suspense*. I'm sure it was because my own mind had done the work of creating the horror. I have occasionally seen Japanese films that come close to reproducing that internal terror but for the most part film doesn't resonate with me that way.

I was born in 1939 in Holywood. No, not *that* Hollywood. Mine, although pronounced the same way, has only one "l": Holywood, County Down, Northern Ireland, situated on the Belfast Lough halfway between Belfast and the town of Bangor. In those days it was a provincial town, almost sleepy, but we knew about our namesake in America. Our cinema got all the movies, two new ones every week, and the comics and the pulp paperbacks were readily available. Radio, though, or "the wireless" as it was called, was completely British.

Radio was a big deal in the wartime years. It comforted, inspired, and kept everyone on a hopeful path. While I don't remember wartime broadcasts clearly, I can only suppose my mother and aunts and grandparents clung to the radio for news of the Blitz and the war effort or the rise and fall of Hitler's fortunes on the continent. I do remember my Mum and Auntie Clara, after weeks of not knowing the whereabouts of Dad and Uncle Bert, hearing their regimental tune, *Lillibulera*, broadcast from England, and concluding with relief that they were safe and sound somewhere near Aldershot.

For me, the most memorable wireless moment was personal and came when I was bitten by the President of the United States. At that time, at three years old, I answered to my christened name "Rosabelle." While visiting a neighbour, I distinctly heard a man's voice in their radio calling my name. I ran over to the console and peered behind it to see what he wanted. I must have touched something, a loose wire or valve, I suppose, and felt a painful jolt. My mother, while she was soothing me, tried to explain that the voice wasn't calling me but was saying the name of President Roosevelt. The more she explained, the more convinced I became that the President himself had called me over with the malicious intention of biting me.

Notwithstanding the episode with Roosevelt, most of my childhood associations with radio were pleasant, especially family gatherings at my grandparents' place. Their home was typical of working-class terrace housing in Ireland, only two rooms on the main floor: the parlour and the living room. The parlour, with its upright piano, lace curtains and plush sofa, and the Big Ben chiming clock on the mantlepiece, was rarely used. All our get-togethers took place in the living room. One side of the room was taken up by a huge black sideboard that displayed my grandmother's treasures: her willow pattern plates and her brass and china souvenirs of important events or past holiday trips—the Lyon's tea caddy, for example, from the World's Fair in London and the little pink mug that boasted McKenna and McGinley Soda Water in spidery black letters. The fireplace was on the opposite side and the dining table took up the rest of the room. Slung high up near the ceiling, was the drying rack, draped with clothing and linen from the latest wash.

In those memories, the radio was always playing. I don't have a distinct recollection of what my grandparents' radio or even our own radio looked like, but I think it's because when we listened, we never actually looked at the radio itself. We would be gathered around the table sharing a meal or nestled in front of the fire, chatting, watching the ever-changing embers, or toasting something on long-handled forks—usually barmbrack, a plump yeasty tea bread dotted with raisins and candied peel, which we consumed with our scant ration of butter.

The songs I recall from that period were those you might expect: "We'll Meet Again," "The White Cliffs of Dover," "Mairzy Doats and Dozy Doats." The comedy shows of the day were popular, and the familiar voices of Tony Hancock and Arthur Askey provoked much laughter and chatter at those fireside gatherings. After a time, my brother and sister and I would be packed upstairs to the third floor where we would lie under the attic skylight drifting off to the faraway music of the radio intermingled with muffled family voices, even now, to my mind, unmatchable as the sound of well-being.

Our first home in Canada was the upper floor of a house in River Canard, Ontario. It was unfurnished, with no running water. Water had to be carried from a pump in the backyard up a flight of rickety wooden steps that led to the second-floor entrance; the outhouse biffy was accessed by those same steps. In the middle of the main room was a pot-bellied coal stove that my mother used for cooking all our meals, the only source of heat.

The job my father thought awaited him in Canada had fallen through, and with some trepidation my parents dipped into their savings to buy two double beds, a few pots and pans, and snowsuits for my brother and sister and me. It was late October and there were already several inches of snow on the ground.

Even with the stove we had trouble keeping warm, so when my sister and I arrived home from school my mother would bundle us and our little brother into one of the beds, set as close to the stove as possible, while she cooked supper. Her resources were limited but I don't remember feeling deprived. There were plenty of those floury concoctions so dear to the British palate: potato bread, soda bread, or scones, and a big pot of lamb stew or beef and barley soup to go with them. And to round out our cuisine there were various canned goods—baked beans, bully beef and beets, which we liked doused in vinegar—and blancmange, jello, custard, and prunes.

The other thing my parents bought at that time was a radio. We were socially isolated those first months, but radio brought us into the fold. My Dad listened avidly to the news. We had a continuous stream of popular songs, shows like *Twenty Questions*, a lot of comedies and, what I liked best, radio dramas: *Lux Radio Theatre*, *The Philip Morris Playhouse*, *The Shadow*, *The Adventures of Superman*, *The Lone Ranger*, *Boston Blackie* and other wisecracking detectives. Because we were just across the border from Detroit, most of the programs we heard were American, originating from that other Hollywood. I don't think much literary merit could be found in any of those shows. They were pulp driven, brassy, crude, and constructed for shock value, but to my nine-year-old soul they were as comforting and necessary as the stews and soda bread my mother produced.

By the following spring my father had found work and he and my mother put a down payment on a house of our own, a two-storey structure with four walls, a roof, and not much else. No rooms, just a labyrinth of two-by-fours where the walls would go. Set seven miles out from the city of Windsor and a mile or two from LaSalle, the nearest town, it seemed even more isolated than our first home. And even more primitive. Like the first, it had no plumbing or heating, but worse, no electricity. *No radio!* Every day my sister and I trudged the long mile from where the school bus dropped us off at our road and as soon as it came into view we would peer anxiously at our house. It was several weeks before we saw the longed-for signal. The porch light was *on*. We were hooked up!

Gradually, through my father's steady labour, the walls went up, rooms were defined, a well was dug, and plumbing installed. More important to my sister and me, we could once again listen to the radio, and though many of the shows were past our bedtime, my mother could be persuaded to turn up the sound. Lying there in the dark just listening was the best. None of those radio plays were great literature. They didn't bathe us in the beauty of language or stir us with insightful observations, they offered cheap thrills. We listened to those gaudy, crude broadcasts and loved every minute of them. The creaking door of *Inner Sanctum*, the creepy mysterious voice of *The Shadow*, the *thump, thump, thump, thump, thumpty-thump* theme music of *The FBI in Peace and War*, which I later learned was from Prokofiev's *The Love for Three Oranges*. Nothing has ever come close to the physical and psychological reaction those shows produced.

What came from all that listening? I remember that sometimes after a broadcast ended, a great restlessness would come over me. My head full of vague unformed questions, I would get out of bed, go to the window, and look out on the neighbours' yard, their unfinished house, their chicken coop, their pump, and farther on the tree-lined ditch where we hunted for tadpoles. Sometimes the moon was out, and everything would have an extra shimmer to it. I can't say that anything profound came to me in those moments of reflection, but eventually the darkness and the shadows and the stars would do their work and my mood would shift into a realm more contemplative and serene.

A few months before we emigrated to Canada, Mahatma Gandhi was assassinated. While we were listening to his funeral on the radio, my mother told me something that was truly astonishing—not only were there people all over the world like us listening to Gandhi's funeral, but some were actually *seeing* it in their homes! A device, she said, like the radio, that could broadcast not only the sounds of the funeral but actual pictures. It was like watching the cinema in your own home. I wondered how that could possibly be.

A year or two after we moved to our new house, people on our street started getting televisions. Before long almost everyone had a set. One family bought two, because there were two channels and they wanted to watch both at once. My parents held out, feeling a TV was unnecessary. Until 1953. In June that year Queen Elizabeth was crowned and one of our neighbours invited us over to watch the coronation. Shortly after that a television set took pride of place in our living room, and eventually its broadcasts completely preempted radio in our lives. But at the beginning, I clearly remember that after the enchantments of radio, television programs—especially theatrical productions—seemed flat and undramatic.

If I have any regrets about that time, it is that we didn't listen to more Canadian radio drama. My mother liked the women's shows that CBC produced, and CBC News was considered by both my parents to be far superior to the American news services. But it was American drama that we inevitably listened to.

We did not know that CBC had been created to draw its widely scattered listeners into a common purpose and single community, relieve their isolation, and make them aware of Canadian concerns and politics. Much as the construction of the Canadian railways had warded off the incursions of the United States and pulled the far flung and sparsely populated country together as a single entity, it was hoped that public radio would counteract the ubiquitous U.S. content and help to create a Canadian identity. Those in rural communities found much that was of value on the CBC: regular up-to-date quotes on prices for stock and grain, weather reports, and other information vital to the successful operation of their farms. In terms of cultural identity, the CBC became an important outlet and showcase for Canadian music and drama, and for many people constituted the only access to literary and musical creations.

It was inevitable that once we acquired a television we were irrevocably severed from radio. When I went to university in the sixties, I once again became radio-dependent and then *did* listen to CBC radio drama—in fact, it was a radio play by Robertson Davies that inspired me to write my first stage play. In this I am not unlike many Canadian writers who found literary inspiration in CBC Radio and later received support from and opportunities to write for the same institution. Once my radio career had started, I listened to all the current radio drama, much of which, like *Vanishing Point*, *Sunday Matinee*, and the daily drama series on *Morningside*, was of high quality.

In the mid-nineties I received a commission to write a 6-episode mystery series for the very popular *Mystery Project*. The super-star of the *Mystery Project* was without question James W. Nichol, whose celebrated *Midnight Cab* ran for 35 episodes. To my mind *Midnight Cab* was the best of the dramas I listened to, projecting the same mysterious tenor and haunting flavour of my early listening experiences. You can imagine how delighted I was to have James as mentor/editor while writing my own series. He was a generous and supportive critic, and I learned a lot about radio writing as he helped me to hone my episodes.

In 1973, the publisher McClelland and Stewart, my husband David's employer, decided to open a Western office, and sent him to be Editor of the new enterprise. We packed all our belongings into our three-quarter ton and headed west. When we first arrived in Alberta we didn't think we'd be staying very long. We came burdened with the typical easterner's assumption that the pioneer West had been a dismal dustbowl, its people overwhelmed and worn down by hard times, and that it wasn't likely that much had changed. We travelled via the Trans-Canada Highway, which—Manitoba onwards—was laid out along the flattest, least complex route possible, and while we were taken with the horizon-to-horizon views and vast skies we weren't overly impressed with the prairies.

Calgary was approaching its centennial year, and our circumstances and work threw us into the memoirs, letters, photographs, and stories of early residents of the province, many of whom we met. We were overwhelmed at the optimism, and general rambunctious and irreverent attitude of virtually everyone we met or read about. We became born-again Albertans and never looked back. This sense of kinship deepened when we drove out into the countryside. We had expected to fall in love with the mountains to the west but, free of the constriction of the Trans-Canada Highway, it was the prairies we bonded with: the rolling vistas, limitless skies, and the light, the glorious prairie light that cast a spell of romance over everything in view. There was rarely a weekend that we didn't head south and east, seeking out little towns with their churches and basilicas and colourful grain elevators, and exploring the sloughs and coulees of the Alberta grasslands.

The office of McClelland and Stewart West was on 8th Avenue. While it isn't particularly relevant to our new Albertan identity, the following makes an interesting radio sidebar. In 1974, the year after we arrived, William Aberhart's Prophetic Bible Institute, located just across the street from M. & S. West, was torn down. This was surprising to us since, only three years before, after nearly four decades, the long-standing Social Credit party relinquished power. Aberhart built the institute in 1927 to house his Bible study school; it was from there that his famous weekly program *Back to the Bible Hour* was broadcast. His charismatic and engaging voice and his messages of hope were a source of comfort to Albertans during the first years of the Depression. Later, his political messages on social credit were received with similar enthusiasm. Aberhart contended that that a surefire way for governments to increase spending and stimulate the economy was to dispense money or "social credit" to its citizens. So effective was he in reaching his audience that in 1935 his Social Credit party overthrew the long-reigning United Farmers of Alberta party. Aberhart died while in office in 1943, and was succeeded by Ernest Manning, who inevitably shifted the party's focus away from his predecessor's economic theories. But Aberhart remains today as the exemplar of someone who used the magnetic power of radio to disseminate and create an audience for his political theories.

My first radio drama was an adaptation of one of my stage plays, *The Chosen*. Producer and director Mark Schoenberg had seen it at the Edmonton Fringe Festival and commissioned me to create a radio adaptation for CBC's *Vanishing Point*, which had been recently created by CBC producer Bill Lane. Falling somewhere between science fiction and horror, *The Chosen* was a nasty little play and if I chuckled evilly to myself when I first wrote it for stage, I chuckled even more when I worked on the radio adaptation. I was to write two more dramas for *Vanishing Point*: *The Man Who Collected Women* and *Do the Baby Last*.

Two commissions for *Morningside*, hosted by Peter Gzowski, followed shortly: *The Benefactor* and *Love and War Western Style*. These, quite different in tone from my *Vanishing Point* plays, drew upon the people and memoirs I'd read when I first came to Calgary. Just about every incident or story idea in *Love and War* came from those memoirs—the criminal peas and stealing chickens with the aid of a heated pole just two. One of the main themes came directly from a fellow whose memories I'd helped edit for one of those local histories so prevalent in Alberta in the eighties. He had many great stories, but what captivated me was the one where he had inadvertently (or so he said) run over his wife in the rain while she was, at his instructions, retrieving a bag of feed from a ditch.

Don't Fence Me In and *The Pretzel Maker* were written a year or two later, and when I put this anthology together it seemed that these two plays went very well with *Love and War Western Style*, even though they were not as realistic. In fact, they were scarcely realistic at all. There are two characters in these plays that I feel are distinctly radio characters: Cornelia the wish therapist in *The Pretzel Maker* and Boss the imaginary horse in *Don't Fence Me In*. It wouldn't be impossible to show the results of Cornelia's clairvoyance and wish-therapy manipulations in a film, but I believe, and I think you will agree when you read the text, that Eric's various Fred Astair metamorphoses and the galloping horse sequence are far better left to listeners' imaginative responses and constructions than to the special effects department of a film studio.

As for Boss in *Don't Fence Me In*, his physical appearance was severely compromised by the inventive limitations of Mitch, the guy who imagined him and who had a sketchy knowledge at best of what a horse was or looked like (he wasn't "a student of horseflesh," as Boss put it). Again, the listener's imagination does a much better job of creating a satisfactory image of Boss than filmic distortion could achieve. Boss is a character created largely by his voice, a "creation" that takes place inside the head of the listener. Where that "voice" came from, with its shifting back and forth between tenses and its nutty take on the world, is a mystery to me. I can only say that at the time I wrote the play, our house was filled with teenaged boys. They were a lively, exuberant lot, with an endless repertoire of jokes and stories. Their language inevitably crept into the script; Boss is definitely a reflection of their wackiness and eccentric humour and their tendency to shift tenses, especially when they were emphasizing a point.

In reading these plays, the reader might question whether or not there really is a style of love peculiar to the West. It is my contention there is—and it is due to the strength of Western women, especially Alberta women. After all, this is the province where in 1927 the Famous Five fought all the way to the Privy Council in Britain to have women declared "persons," a decision that had positive repercussions for women all over the British Commonwealth, removing many of the barriers that held women back, and forever changing the way women were thought of and treated.

Love and War Western Style not only reflects the exuberance and optimism that we were so impressed with in pioneer memoirs, its persistent feminist thread draws on the resilience and self-determination of Alberta women. Thighbone, the setting of *Love and War*, is a town where "the men are tough but the women are tougher." They are also resourceful and independent-minded. The women in the other contributions to this anthology—Effie in *Don't Fence Me In* and Cornelia in *The Pretzel Maker*—demonstrate the same qualities. While romantic traditions and expectations are not always followed, there is plenty of romance going on for these women, always on their own terms.

It has been fun for me to revisit these plays and draw them together as a book. I hope it will be fun for those who read it, and an opportunity as well to explore what has become a vanishing art form in Canada. Very little radio drama can be found now, at least on traditional broadcasting. The CBC no longer produces it. However, with the possibilities offered by the internet and so many technical developments in digital media, many young artists are experimenting with the form. There are a multitude of podcasts, many of which feature radio plays. So, it is not unreasonable to assume there could well be a renaissance in aural drama.

The plays in *Love and War Western Style* were my response not only to the extreme friendliness of the west, but to the optimism and irreverence that we found on our arrival in Alberta over fifty years ago. I can't claim that optimism and irreverence are unique to my dramas, but I do feel that in these times of polarization and the danger involved in sending up the status quo that there is a serious need for more frequent exploration of these themes.

DON'T FENCE ME IN

Don't Fence Me In was commissioned by Studio 92, CBC, and aired in January 1992. Series producer Bill Lane.

Produced and directed by	MARTIE FISHMAN
Recording Engineer	ROBERT DOBLE
Sound Effects Technician	UTE SCHAFFLAND
Production Assistant	CHRISTINE STOREY
Composer/Keyboards	RON CASAT
Guitar	TIM WILLIAMS

CAST:

Richard Newman	BOSS
Grant Reddick	MITCH
Joyce Doolittle	EFFIE
Brian Jensen	KINCAID
Stephen Sparks	BAD GUY ONE
John Hudson	BAD GUY TWO
Jim Leyden	CITIZEN
Gordon Signer	JACKSON
Lisa Bunting	SHADY LADY/PALOMINO

CAST OF CHARACTERS

According to *Boss*—his imaginary horse—*Mitch Carter* has the perfect life. He spends his days and nights dreaming up western plots where he and *Boss* ride from one small town to another rescuing good and simple folk like *Jackson* and *Citizen* from the predatory grip of the villainous *Dan Kincaid* and his seedy sidekicks *Bad Guy One, Bad Guy Two* and *Shady Lady.* But things go terribly wrong when Mitch's old friend *Effie* moves in. As Boss puts it, Effie couldn't be in your presence more than two minutes before she was bossing you around and ripping your life out from under you and plumping it up and banging it about like one of those decorator pillows. Before long Effie has invaded not only Mitch's house but his dreams as well, with disastrous results. Even her imaginary horse *Palomina* is pushy and obstinate.

SCENE ONE

TWANGY WESTERN VOICE SINGS "DON'T FENCE ME IN."

APPROACHING HOOFBEATS.

GENERAL HUBBUB, FOLKS TALKING EXCITEDLY, "IT'S MITCH CARTER." "KINCAID BETTER WATCH OUT." "MITCH'LL FIX 'IM."

SCENE TWO

ROOM ABOVE THE SALOON: CARD PLAYING. DRINKING. THE OUTSIDE HUBBUB IS FAINTLY AUDIBLE.

BAD GUY ONE: What's going on out there?

BAD GUY TWO: Stranger riding into town on a yeller horse.

SHADY LADY: Lemme see. Hey! Don't you know who that is? That's Mitch Carter.

BAD GUY ONE: Mitch Carter! Someone better tell Dan Kincaid.

BAD GUY TWO: What's all the fuss? Looks like an ordinary kinda guy to me.

SHADY LADY: That shows how much you know.

BAD GUY TWO: I like his horse.

WHINNY!

BOSS: (CONFIDENTIALLY.) That horse he's talking about? That's me, Mitch's horse. Boss. Short for Boscoe. Genuine Indian paint, yellow with brown and black patches. I've never known mother or father 'cause Mitch never bothered to dream me up any. Mitch says I'm the best. Well okay, physically there might be some argument. Mitch was never a student of horseflesh and if you look at me from some angles, I'm a little off kilter. But heck, who cares what they look like when they can outrun anything that moves. Mitch and me have outrun trains, cars, runaway stages, jumped off cliffs. Okay so my ears're too short and my tail's a little stubby, but when it comes to heart, I'm unbeatable, eh? I'm a *man's* horse.

HORSEY SOBS.

BOSS: I know, I know. A *man's* horse wouldn't cry. But what am I supposed to do? An imaginary feller can't go on if someone won't imagine him, no matter how goldarn manly he is.

MORE HORSEY SOBS.

BOSS: It's all Effie's fault. We wouldn't be having this problem if Effie hadn't gone and bumped off Dan Kincaid . . . 'Scuse me. I just got all overcome for a moment. What you have to know is that Mitch is a guy with an obsession, and what he's obsessed with is the Western Dream. He spends his days and nights dreaming up western movie plots with him as the hero . . . And *me* as his horse.

SCENE THREE

UNDERLYING SOUND OF GOOD AND SIMPLE FOLK. KIDS PLAYING. DOGS BARKING.

BOSS: Okay now, I gotta tell you Mitch's fantasies are pretty simple. They all take place in little one-horse towns called, Gunshot, or Abaloney, or Mesquite, and the folk of these towns are all simple, good folk. Their sons are good and simple, and their daughters are good and simple too, besides being pretty as daisies in a dung heap.

CITIZEN: Howdy, Jackson.

JACKSON: Howdy, yourself.

CITIZEN: How's the missus?

JACKSON: Missus is fine, and yours?

CITIZEN: Never better. How's them kids of yours?

JACKSON: Kids is fine, just fine. How about yours?

CITIZEN: My kids? Well, my kids are . . . uh . . . well, they're fine.

BOSS: As I said, good and simple. And good and simple it would stay if it wasn't for Dan Kincaid. He gets his evil grip on one of those innocent little towns and next thing you know those good and simple folk are suffering, and getting ruined, and getting picked off like flies.

PILLAGE, GUNFIRE, MAYHEM, CRIES OF ANGUISH!

BOSS: This is the point at which Mitch and me ride into town. Mitch takes a look around, sizes up the situation, and, before you know it, he makes Dan Kincaid clean up his act.

DOOR OF SALOON PUSHED OPEN. DEN OF SIN SOUNDS.

MITCH: All right Kincaid, you low down, thieving snake!

KINCAID: You talking to me, Pill Face?

MITCH: I'm gonna kick your side-winding butt outta town.

KINCAID: (TRIES TO SUPPRESS A LAUGH.) Pbbh! Yeah, right!

BAD GUY CHUCKLES.

MITCH: You've been carrying on your evil ways long enough.

KINCAID: You mean there's a time limit?

BAD GUY GUFFAWS!

MITCH: You son of a snake. I'm gonna fix your wagon.

KINCAID: Suits me. I've enjoyed about as much of this conversation as I can stand.

FIGHTING, AND NOISY SUPPORT OF KINCAID BY HIS MEN.

MITCH: Had enough, Kincaid?

KINCAID: (BRUISED AND BROKEN.) You ain't heard the last of this, Carter.

BAD GUY ONE: Come on, Kincaid. Let's get outta here.

KINCAID: (FADING OFF.) You'd better be hoping our paths don't cross, Carter.

BOSS: And Kincaid would go. And then Mitch and me would ride out of town. And that would be the end of it.

RIDING OUT OF TOWN. WESTERN MUSIC. "HAPPY TRAILS TO YOU."

BOSS: But that wouldn't be the end of it, eh? Sure as shooting the next town we came to Dan Kincaid would be there, running a bank scam, or some kind of cattle rustling ring, or something that put all the daughters in jeopardy. But no matter how clever and wicked Kincaid was, Mitch would always whip him.

MITCH: You get your butt outta town, Kincaid, and keep it out.

KINCAID: You got me this time, Mitch, but you'd better keep a lookout over your shoulder from now on.

MITCH: Why? Is the boogeyman gonna get me?

BOSS: You get the idea? Okay so that's the way it was—everything just ambling along—with Mitch dreaming up all sorts of great adventures and me and him mopping up the west . . . Until a few weeks back.

SCENE FOUR

DING DONG.

BOSS: He never should have answered that door.

HAMMERING ON DOOR!

MITCH: I'm coming. Keep your shirt on!

DOOR OPENING.

EFFIE: Hi, Mitch.

MITCH: Effie? What are you doing here?

EFFIE: It's Boyd. You heard he left me?

MITCH: Yep. I believe I did hear something.

EFFIE: Well, the old goat has sold the house out from under me. I need a place to stay for a few days.

MITCH: Gee, I wish I could help you, Effie, but there's no room.

EFFIE: There's plenty of room. Unless you've been taking in boarders. You got three bedrooms. As I recall.

MITCH: Yes, but . . .

EFFIE: Now Mitch. When Dora walked out, we put you up.

MITCH: And we were about ready to murder each other, too.

EFFIE: We're kissing cousins, for Pete's sake. You can put me up for a day or two, till I find my feet. Give me a hand with these cases.

HELPING EFFIE IN WITH THE CASES.

MITCH: So why did Boyd walk out, anyways?

EFFIE: Dora . . . Ughhh. You still smoking those stogies?

MITCH: Boyd and Dora? My Dora?

EFFIE: She's Boyd's Dora now. It smells like a train station in here. Don't you ever open a window?

OPENING WINDOW.

MITCH: Effie, I really don't think this'll work out.

EFFIE: What's to work out? I'm only staying for a couple of weeks. Till I find a place of my own.

MITCH: What about your kids?

EFFIE: Did you stay with your kids?

MITCH: I couldn't. They sympathized with Dora.

EFFIE: Yeah. Well, mine sympathize with Boyd.

MITCH: Boyd and Dora! I can't believe it.

EFFIE: Yeah. Well, you won't hear me humming, "Love is a many splendoured thing."

SCENE FIVE

BOSS: To say that we were worried about Effie moving in, would be like saying a chicken was worried about a coyote taking up residence in the coop. Effie couldn't be in your presence more than two minutes before she was bossing you around and ripping your life out from under you and plumping it up and banging it about like one of those decorator pillows.

MITCH: (MUSING.) She's good looking, I'll give her that. In her salad days Effie was pretty as a toothpaste ad.

BOSS: (SNORT. SPEAKS UNDER HIS BREATH.) With a mouth on her like a teamster and the personality to match.

MITCH: (MUSING.) Even now she's a fine-looking woman.

BOSS: (SNORTS AGAIN.) If she'd shut up for five minutes in a row you could almost bear her company. (SIGHS.) The first couple of days didn't go so badly. Whenever Effie'd start in on him, Mitch'd just settle down with a stogie and drive her out of the room. Then me and him could get on with business. I already told you his specialty was cleaning up one horse towns. The people of these little places all understood Mitch's philosophy.

SCENE SIX

SALOON SOUNDS, DRINKS CLINKING, PIANO, SINGER.

JACKSON: I heard this Mitch feller has a special feeling for little places like ours.

CITIZEN: Fill 'er up, Jackson. How d'ya mean *special feeling*?

GLASS CLUNKING ON THE BAR AND DRINK POURING.

JACKSON: Well just that he figures anything bigger, the people are sophisticated and decadent and deserve what they get, but in little towns the folks is naive and genuine and deserving of saving.

CITIZEN: A man with a mission, eh?

JACKSON: Yep. Only Mitch is not your usual hero. He's more a regular guy that you don't even suspect is a hero till you see him riding off into the sunset and you realize this man has saved your whole town and made it safe for your wife and children and you didn't even get a good look at his face.

BOSS: He was right. Mitch don't look like your usual hero. He always wears this old dark dusty jacket like Walter Huston wore in *Law and Order*. His hands are clean but rough from doing a man's work and he speaks real quiet, which makes some people underestimate him. But they always live to regret it. Course now, Effie couldn't be expected to understand any of this. She'd never spot the heroic side of a guy like Mitch.

EFFIE: You know, Mitch. I never noticed before, but you tilt a bit to one side like a bent bean pole.

BOSS: How could she see a hero in someone she obviously considered a slob and a dolt?

EFFIE: You know, Mitch, you've *got* to give up nicotine. Your fingers are all yellow from those smokes.

BOSS: See what I mean?

SCENE SEVEN

VACUUMING, WRENCHING A JOINT, CLANKING, HAMMERING TACKS, SAWING BOARDS, HAMMERING ON ROOF.

BOSS: Effie hadn't even settled in before she took over the place like she owned it, working up a storm till everything was finger-licking clean.

After the cleaning came the fixing. She fixed all the leaky taps and squeaky hinges. She put new carpet on the steps to the basement, nailed down the loose boards on the front porch, painted the fence. She even fixed the roof.

MITCH: You don't have to do that, you know.

EFFIE: (FROM THE ROOF.) Somebody has to do it.

MITCH: I don't see why you're fussing so much when you're only going to be here a couple of weeks.

EFFIE: I am *looking*, if that's what you mean.

FLURRY OF HAMMERING.

MITCH: That's not what I mean. You don't have to get testy.

EFFIE: I was out this morning. Every place I looked at was either too crappy or too expensive.

MITCH: I didn't mean that. Take as long as you want. I just don't see why you have to do all this work.

EFFIE: I like to earn my keep.

CLATTERING.

MITCH: You're gonna break your neck, up there.

EFFIE: So?

MITCH: So right. What am *I* worried for?

EFFIE: Listen, I could be lured down from here.

MITCH: Oh yeah?

EFFIE: All this work sure makes a gal hungry.

MITCH: Oh yeah?

SCENE EIGHT

CLINKING DISHES IN KITCHEN.

EFFIE: Oh wow! Mushrooms, tomatoes. My omelets are like eating paper plates.

MITCH: I know.

EFFIE: (LAUGHS.) Anything I cook should come with a Surgeon General's warning. I think that's why Boyd left me.

MITCH: Don't blame him.

EFFIE: I'm good at fixing things though.

MITCH: Yeah, I noticed. About all I can fix is a scotch and soda.

EFFIE: But you sure can cook.

MITCH: Maybe Boyd shoulda run off with me.

EFFIE BREAKS OUT IN A FIT OF LAUGHTER. MITCH JOINS IN.

BOSS: Sound really pally, don't they? It's all part of her plan. What she's doing, see, is undermining Mitch's manhood. The way I figure, Effie is one of these superwomen, one of the new feminists, that wants to take on all the man-type work and leave the female kind of stuff to the men.

Now don't get me wrong. There's nothing wrong with men cooking. They have to do it on the trail. Mitch was always a good cook, but he used to cook man-type stuff, beans and sausages and flapjacks. He wouldn't have been caught dead cooking an omelet before Effie nosied her way in.

SCENE NINE

EFFIE: Mitch! Are you going to sit there and smoke those things all day? Why don't you get off your butt and do something!

MITCH: Like what?

EFFIE: Well, I don't know. What would you be doing if I wasn't here?

MITCH: I'd be at the races.

EFFIE: Well, what are we waiting for?

BOSS: Sounds good, eh? Do they sound compatible or what? Wrong!

SCENE TEN

AT THE RACES. WINNING SOUNDS.

BOSS: Effie went to the races, which was something Dora wouldn't have done in a million years. But there was no joy in it for Mitch. He lost forty bucks in the first hour and Effie made a hundred and sixty. She mopped up.

EFFIE: Yahoo! Another fifty bucks.

MITCH: Why is it that whatever horse you take a fancy to comes barreling in two lengths ahead of the field?

EFFIE: I know my horses, Mitch.

MITCH: So, who do you pick for the next race?

EFFIE: Bus Boy.

MITCH: Bus Boy! Gimme a break. Jerry's Folly. Jerry's Folly's a shoe-in.

EFFIE: You could make a fortune on this one. I'm betting the day's winnings on him.

MITCH: He'll never beat Jerry's Folly.

EFFIE: Have it your way.

RACE SOUNDS COME IN AND CONTINUE.

MITCH: I will. Believe me.

EFFIE: What's happening? Can you see?

MITCH: Jerry's Folly leading the field.

EFFIE: Here, gimme those binoculars. Yeah, he's in front, but he's easily winded. You'll see.

MITCH: He's pulled ahead another length. So how much did you bet on that clunker?

EFFIE: Come on, Bus Boy. Show your stuff! Bus Boy! Bus Boy!

MITCH: (LAUGHS.) You're wasting your time.

EFFIE: Oh yeah? Look at that.

MITCH: I don't believe it! I don't believe it! Look at that sucker go!

EFFIE: Come on Bus Boy! Come on Bus Boy! (GOES WILD, WHOOPING AND CHEERING, ENDING WITH A BIG "HEE HAW!") Do I know how to pick 'em?

MITCH: You sure do. Next time I'll listen.

BOSS: Okay, so Mitch is the kind of guy puts a good face on things, no matter how much he's hurting. But inside you could bet that Effie was undermining his morale.

But that wasn't the worst. Up till the races all she'd done was mess around with his *reality*. The worst was yet to come.

SCENE ELEVEN

HOOVES CLOPPING AND TRAIL MUSIC.

BOSS: Okay, here's how it started. Mitch and me are riding towards the town of Crystal Butte, when we're met by a good citizen of the town. It was the usual situation. Kincaid had taken over Crystal Butte and was scamming all the good and simple people of the town out of their life savings and all their dreams were shriveling up and dying off.

CITIZEN: You wouldn't believe how bad it is, Mr. Carter. Women in spangly dresses parading their wares right out on the street. Drunks fighting and shooting the place up. And you should see what they've done to the saloon. Used to be a real nice place. You could get your morning shave there, drink a few beers and chew the rag with the fellas. Now it's a gambling den downstairs, with loose women and who knows what upstairs.

MITCH: Sounds bad.

CITIZEN: I'll say! Gangsters and gun men from the whole territory are riding in every day. It's a mean and dangerous situation, the kind that would take the cavalry and the militia together to fix.

MITCH: You just leave it in my hands. I'll take care of everything. Now . . . The first thing we gotta do is find us a pump.

CITIZEN: A pump? Iffen yore thirsty I can . . .

MITCH: Nope. A pump'll do just fine.

CITIZEN: There's a pump in the school yard at the end of the street there. But watch out for the school marm. She's as upright as a cactus and twice as prickly.

KIDS IN THE SCHOOL YARD.

BOSS: So, Mitch gets himself over to the school yard. By this time a passel of bad guys have heard about him and followed him to the pump.

BAD GUY SOUNDS.

BOSS: Okay, so Mitch knows this eh? He planned it! He dismounts in plain view of everyone and pumps himself a dipperful of water.

PUMP HANDLE RISING AND FALLING.

SHADY LADY: What's he doing?

BAD GUY ONE: He's getting a drink of water.

SHADY LADY: Water's for sissies and kids.

MITCH, SPITTING OUT WATER.

BAD GUY ONE: Oops. He don't like that water much. He's spitting it out. Watch out, he's pulling his gun!

MITCH SHOOTING THE PUMP. GASPS!
EXCLAMATIONS OF "HE'S SHOOTING THE PUMP!"

SHADY LADY: What's he doing that for?

BAD GUY ONE: Guess he didn't like the taste of the water . . . or the looks of the pump.

SHADY LADY: He's crazy!

SHOOTING THE PUMP AGAIN.

BAD GUY ONE: Guess I'll mosey on back to the saloon.

SHADY LADY: Wait for me!

BOSS: Mitch took his time getting back in the saddle. By then the ruffians had all vanished and the kids had run back in the schoolhouse. We could see the school marm looking out the window at us. There was an oddly familiar look to her, but we didn't dwell on the fact.

CLOPPING SOUNDS.

BOSS: We trotted back down the main street and when we got to the saloon, Mitch got down and tied me to the railing.

MITCH: Now Boss, old feller, you wait here. I got a little business inside.

BOSS: He gave me a pat and pushed his way through the swinging doors of the saloon.

SCENE TWELVE

SALOON SOUNDS.

BOSS: Okay, so I wasn't just going to stand there, right? I pulled the reins free and got up on the sidewalk and looked in over the saloon doors. Pretty near everyone in town was there. And it was obvious that they'd all heard about Mitch and the pump.

BAD GUY ONE: Looky there. That there's the man who shot the pump.

BAD GUY TWO: He looks like a quiet enough feller.

BAD GUY ONE: You shoulda seen him shoot that pump. Nothing quiet about it.

BAD GUY TWO: All the same, he looks like a regular feller.

JACKSON: What can I get you sir?

MITCH: Glass of water.

EVERYONE: Water? Did he say Water?

BAD GUY TWO: I wouldn't want to be in Jackson's shoes right now.

BOSS: Jackson the barkeep's hand trembled as he poured the water. He looked at the glass before he gave it to Mitch, decided it wasn't clean enough and poured another.

JACKSON: There you are, Mister. Drink it in good health.

BOSS: Mitch took a sip of water and rolled it around his tongue. Everyone in the place was watching. You could have heard a feather drop.

FEATHER DROPPING.

BOSS: He paused a moment, drained the glass in one long swallow. Then he throws a big silver dollar on the counter.

GUZZLING WATER AND SMACKING LIPS.
CLINKING COIN.
GENERAL SIGH OF RELIEF.

MITCH: Fine water, son.

BOSS: It was then that I noticed him. Over in a dark corner of the saloon playing cards. Stocky, big chested, big gold watch on a chain. Hands smooth and manicured, sporting a diamond ring the size of an ice cube. *Dan Kincaid.*

KINCAID: Who's that feller at the bar?

BAD GUY TWO: That's the feller shot the pump, Mr. Kincaid.

SHADY LADY: Don't mess with him Dan. He's dangerous.

KINCAID: He don't frighten me none. Ask him over here.

LAUGHTER OF HARD-DRINKING, DEBAUCHED MEN.

BOSS: Okay, so Kincaid's flunky passes on the invitation to Mitch. And Mitch? He brushes past him like he was a fly or something and pushes through the swinging doors into the sunshine. Behind him, Dan Kincaid turns dark red. You know that this insult from Mitch has cut deep, and Kincaid won't rest till the score has been settled. But the rage of Dan Kincaid was nothing to the trouble that was waiting outside.

SCENE THIRTEEN

MITCH: Boss. What have I told you about eavesdropping?

WHINNY AND CLATTER OF HOOVES.

MITCH: Nobody likes a nosy horse.

BOSS: (SNORT.)

EFFIE CALLING IN THE DISTANCE.

MITCH: Hey mister, who's that lady over there? That one. Pretty as a toothpaste ad, ain't she?

CITIZEN: Oh, you don't want to mess with her. That's the school marm. Mouth like a mule driver.

EFFIE: (AS SCHOOL MARM, SLIGHTLY CLOSER.) You! You there!

MITCH: The school teacher? I think she's trying to get my attention. She . . . looks familiar.

BOSS: I couldn't believe my eyes! Darned if it wasn't that Effie horning in on Mitch's dream!

MITCH: How come she's all riled up? Does she need help?

CITIZEN: No sir. She don't need no help. Whoever she's after is gonna need help and that's you buddy. She's looking for the man who shot her pump.

EFFIE: Hey! You're the one who shot my pump! You're going to pay!

MITCH: Boscoe, I think it's time to lope on outta here.

CLOPPING AND MUSIC "MULE TRAIN."

EFFIE: (FADING OFF.) What kind of example . . . Hey! Wait! Come back here!

BOSS: Okay, so that time we were able to avoid her. But the damage was done. From then on whenever Mitch dreamed up an adventure, there Effie was bang in the middle of it, usually as the school marm. And no matter what was happening, she would meddle in it. Pretty soon she began taking over Mitch's job. Pretty soon it was Effie who was cleaning out the dens of sin and rounding up the cattle rustlers and bank robbers.

It got so that by the time Mitch and me rode into a town it was more or less cleaned up. There was nothing left for us to do. Then one day we rode into the town of Pickle Creek . . .

TOWN BEING TORN UP, PAINTED RED AND SENT TO THE DEVIL.

SCENE FOURTEEN

MITCH: Looks like your town's in bad trouble, Mister.

CITIZEN: Yep, Stranger. Pickle Creek's gone about as far downhill as a town can go. The men are whipped and beaten. The women are afraid for their virtue and the babies are getting all pale 'cause their mamas don't dare bring 'em outside.

MITCH: Dan Kincaid?

CITIZEN: How did you know?

SHOOTING AND SHOUTING.

MITCH: What's that?

CITIZEN: Something's being robbed, more'n likely. Must be the hat shop. That's about all that's left.

MITCH: Where's the school marm?

CITIZEN: Tied to the railway tracks. She got uppity with Kincaid once too often.

MITCH: I'd better see to her.

CITIZEN: She's in no immediate danger. The train's not due here till Wednesday.

MITCH: In that case, I'll look up Mr. Kincaid.

CITIZEN: Try the bank.

SCENE FIFTEEN

SUSPENSEFUL MUSIC.

BOSS: The bank was quiet as a funeral parlour. The only person in there, and I know this 'cause I was peeking in through the open window, was the banker, who I recognized as one of Kincaid's men. Mitch strolled casually over to his desk. The banker's forehead was beaded with sweat.

MITCH: Where's Kincaid?

BAD GUY TWO: I . . . I . . . dunno!

MITCH: I'm looking down at your desk, pardner. Besides this here calendar, I see paper, lots of paper, and a whole bunch of well chewed pencils.

BAD GUY TWO: Oh y-y-yeah?

MITCH: And you know what these chewed over pencils tell me? They tell me you're afeared of something. Where is he?

BAD GUY TWO: Ahh! (CHOKING.) Don't! Let me go!

KINCAID: You looking for me? Or you looking for the schoolmarm? (EVIL LAUGH.)

BOSS: Mitch looks at Kincaid. He looks down at the desk. All of a sudden he understands why the banker is sweating and why Kincaid looks so pleased with himself. The calendar on the desk says Wednesday, August Third.

TRAIN WHISTLE.

MITCH: Wednesday! The train! Effie! I've got to get to her!

CHUFFING AND WHISTLE AS TRAIN PULLS INTO TOWN.

KINCAID: Too late. She was tied up on the trestle and the train always whistles after it crosses the trestle. She's done for. And so are you. Hand's up sucker!

GUN DRAWN AND PRIMED.

KINCAID: I think this is going to be the most satisfying day of my life.

EFFIE: (ENTERING.) Think again, meathead!

BOSS: I couldn't believe my eyes! There, standing in the doorway, fresh as a daisy with eyes the colour and sparkle of sarsaparilla and skin as smooth and creamy as a peach sundae was Effie. Holding a gun. She raised it up and drilled three neat holes in Kincaid's chest.

BANG! BANG! BANG!

BOSS: Kincaid clutched at his chest and turned the colour of a boiled shirt. He lunged forward, knocking over a chair and a lamp and, gasping like a gaffed fish, went lurching out into the street.

LURCHING STEPS AND GROANS OF KINCAID, MORTALLY STRUCK.

BOSS: Everyone in town came running to see the spectacle of their oppressor spinning about in his death agonies. He was a long time dying.

THE CONTINUING DEATH OF DAN KINCAID.

MITCH: What'd you do that for?

EFFIE: What!

MITCH: Why'd you shoot Kincaid?

EFFIE: I saved your life!

MITCH: And that's another thing. I'm supposed to save *your* life, dammit.

DAN FINALLY KICKS THE BUCKET.
GASP FROM CROWD.

MITCH: There. See what you've done?

EFFIE: What have I done?

BOSS: Okay, so you really couldn't expect Effie to realize what she'd done. I mean Kincaid was to Mitch what Moriarty was to Sherlock Holmes. Without Kincaid making a mess there was nothing for Mitch to clean up. Anyways, now that Kincaid's gone, there isn't any reason for us to go on. Mitch just sits there moping and I've been put out to pasture. I mean it's a nice pasture with a mountain view and lots of tasty grass—Mitch always gives me the best. But I miss the action. I'm too young to be put out to pasture. Goldarn it. (SOB.)

SCENE SIXTEEN

EFFIE: So, Mitch.

MITCH: (COMING OUT OF HIS REVERIE.) Uh? Yeah?

EFFIE: I found a place. It's not too bad. It's over on . . .

MITCH: Yeah, I saw you packing. I'm not surprised. Must seem pretty tame around here to you.

EFFIE: No! Why would you say that? I just thought it was about time to move on.

MITCH: I guess.

EFFIE: I got you a present.

UNWRAPPING.

MITCH: Gees, Effie. You didn't have to . . . What's this?

EFFIE: It's spurs.

MITCH: I know it's spurs. (EMOTIONAL SILENCE.) They're real nice, Effie. Looks like solid silver.

EFFIE: Yeah. I know it's dumb when you don't even have a horse. But I always sorta thought of you as a kind of, well as a . . . a cowboy?

MITCH: No kidding!

EFFIE: Not one of those goopy types like John Wayne. More like, well did you ever see Walter Huston in *Law and Order*?

MITCH: No kidding!!!

SCENE SEVENTEEN

BOSS: Does she know what buttons to press? It's disgusting. So, she's staying. Yeah, that's right. She's outside right now, fixing his car. He's cooking up some gourmet . . . mess. And I'm stuck here in this blasted field for the rest of my days.

Oh-oh, here he comes. I guess he's feeling guilty about me. Oh no! Does *she* have to be here?

MITCH: You really fixed Kincaid's wagon, Effie.

EFFIE: Had to be done, Mitch.

MITCH: There's a lot more needs fixing out there, Effie.

EFFIE: I'm your fixer.

MITCH: You sure are.

BOSS: Oh yuck! Spare me!

MITCH: I got you a present.

EFFIE: Really? What?

MITCH: Over there. By the cottonwoods.

EFFIE: Oh Mitch! A palomino!

FEMININE WHINNY.

EFFIE: Look at her, that silver white mane and those creamy golden flanks. She's a honey!

APPROACHING HORSE.

BOSS: I'll say! Hubba-hubba! Well, hello sweet thing.

PALOMINA: Keep your sweet talk to yourself. There's work to do, Buddy.

BOSS: The name's Boscoe. Boss for short.

PALOMINA: Well, you're not the boss of me, and don't forget it.

BOSS: They make a nice-looking couple, don't they, Mitch and Effie?

PALOMINA: Wish we could say the same.

BOSS: What's wrong with us?

PALOMINA: Well. How come you're all lopsided?

BOSS: Hey! I'm a man's horse. I can outrun anything that moves.

PALOMINA: You can't outrun me.

BOSS: Can too.

PALOMINA: Wanna bet?

GALLOPING AWAY.

BOSS: She's probably right. She's streaking along like a comet. I'll never catch her up.

But it's sure gonna be fun trying.

GALLOPING AND RAUCOUS MUSIC "MULE TRAIN" GRADUALLY FADES OUT.

THE PRETZEL MAKER

The Pretzel Maker was commissioned by CBC and broadcast live from a tea dance at the Palliser Hotel in 1994. It aired on CBC's Homestretch.

Produced and directed by	MARTIE FISHMAN
Recording Engineer	ROBERT DOBLE
Sound Effects Technician	UTE SCHAFFLAND
Production Assistant	CHRISTINE STOREY

CAST

Brian Jensen	ROCKY
Heather Lea Maccallum	KELLY

CAST OF CHARACTERS

Eric Brownstone, incurable wallflower, is at the Palliser tea dance, hiding behind his teacup, trying to get up the courage to ask someone to dance, when *Cornelia*, self-professed "wish therapist," reads his teacup and unlocks his inner Fred Astaire. When he bumps into beautiful red-haired *Kelly*, who happens to look just like Ginger Rogers, his hairline rolls back like a sardine tin, his feet shrink to nine double A, and he's seized with an irresistible passion for putting on the ritz. It would all be perfect if it wasn't for Kelly's boyfriend *Rocky*—the *Pretzel Maker.*

SCENE ONE

PARTYING, MUSIC, DANCING CROWD, GENTLE CHINKING OF CUPS.

CORNELIA ARRIVING NOISILY AND SITTING IN CHAIR.

CORNELIA: (APPROACHING.) Excuse me. Can I squeeze through here? Do you mind? Whff! What a fanny bumper. I had no idea it would be so packed!

ERIC: Excuse me. This table is taken.

CORNELIA: You *are* Eric Brownstone, aren't you?

ERIC: How did you know?

CORNELIA: I'm a mind reader, right? Well actually a *clairvoyant*. I have a card here somewhere. Anyway, to cut to the chase, I'm here to read your teacup.

ERIC: In that outfit?

CORNELIA: I suppose you want a turban and dangling earrings.

ERIC: If you're happy in leather and fishnets that's ok by me. Just wear them at another table.

CORNELIA RUMMAGING THROUGH HER BAG.

CORNELIA: Didn't you hear me? I'm here to do your *leaves*. Ah! Here it is. Keep this on file. You may want me again.

ERIC: This is the weirdest business card I've ever seen. (READS.) Cornelia Mistral. Soothsayer and . . . Wish Therapist?

CORNELIA: I don't just read the leaves, I "arrange" them as well. It's not conscious. I sit here in your presence, and I twirl the cup around in the saucer, and I kind of act like a lightning rod for your suppressed wishes. And, believe me, you're suppressed. There're some wicked vibes reaching out to me from your little libido.

ERIC: My mother sent you, didn't she?

CORNELIA: No.

ERIC: It's just the sort of ditsy thing she'd do.

CORNELIA: She's right to worry about you.

ERIC: She *did* send you.

CORNELIA: No. Not that I'd blame her. Thirty-five and not married, any mother would worry. Give me your cup.

ERIC: No way.

CORNELIA: Look at you! Chandeliers, flowers, hot music, and you're drinking tea.

ERIC: This *is* a tea dance.

CORNELIA: But don't worry. I'm here to change all that. Put a little aerobic zing in your life. Give me your cup.

ERIC: No.

CORNELIA: It's been written that I shall read your cup at this very moment in time so all the "Nos" in the world won't make a bit of difference.

ERIC: Written where? Keep away!

CORNELIA: Give me that!

ERIC: No!

CORNELIA: I'm taking it. Urgmmphh!

THEY STRUGGLE OVER THE CUP. CHINKING CHINA.

ERIC: No! You're not! Ow! Keep away!

CORNELIA: Give me that. Ughh! One, get away. Two. Don't try and stop me. Three!

AS THEY STRUGGLE, WE HEAR THREE SCRAPES OF THE CUP.

CORNELIA: Ohhhh! Now look what you made me do. It's supposed to turn *clockwise*. Three times in a *clockwise* direction. You've made it go *counter*clockwise!

ERIC: So big deal. Turn it back.

CORNELIA: It can't be turned back. It can't be reversed. You'll have to take what you get and don't blame me if you don't like it.

ERIC: As if I care.

CORNELIA: Oh, you'll care. You'll definitely care. (SIGHS.) It was going to be such a nice read. A charming waltz, a saucy blonde and thou tripping the light fantastic. Now it could be anything. Counterclockwise! *Scary* . . . Oh well. Better see what it says . . . Hmmm . . . Well, well, *well*.

ERIC: What? What do you see in there?

CORNELIA: This is a *kick*!

ERIC: It's just a teacup . . . Are you going to read it to me or not?

CORNELIA: I certainly am. Listen up. Exactly two minutes from now, a woman is going to bump into your table and . . . spill her tea all over you.

ERIC: Great. I can hardly wait.

CORNELIA: She's stunning!

ERIC: Really.

CORNELIA: Flaming red hair . . . white sequinned dress. She looks like Ginger Rogers. You . . . *leap* out of your seat and *grab* her round the waist!

ERIC: As if.

CORNELIA: You are possessed by the spirit of Fred Astaire. Your hair line recedes. Your feet shrink to nine double A. You have an irresistible urge to put on the Ritz.

ERIC: And then?

CORNELIA: I dunno. It gets a little murky . . . Ummm . . . I see a horse . . .

ERIC: A horse?

CORNELIA: (DEFENSIVE.) Yes, a horse. And a . . . pretzel maker?

ERIC: Look could I have my cup back. (POURS HIMSELF MORE TEA.) Look at this. The pot's cold. I'm going to have to order more.

CORNELIA: You don't have time. You need to prepare yourself.

ERIC: Prepare myself to dance with a girl like Ginger Rogers. *Right.*

CORNELIA: It will happen in about . . . thirty seconds.

ERIC: It won't happen if I'm not here.

CORNELIA: What do you mean? Where are you going?

ERIC: It's been nice knowing you. Bye.

CORNELIA: Watch out!!

KELLY BUMPS INTO ERIC, SPILLING TEA ALL OVER HIM.

KELLY: Oh! Ohh! I'm so sorry! Here, let me wipe that up.

ERIC: *Wow* . . . You look like . . . I don't . . . *Holy crumoly*! (MAKES STRANGE NOISES OF METAMORPHOSIS.) My *feet!*

KELLY: Did I spill some on your shoes?

METAMORPHIC SOUNDS CONTINUE.

ERIC: No. My feet are . . . Wooh . . . kind of . . . Yipes . . . nimbling up!

KELLY: (SURPRISE AND DELIGHT.) Oh!

ERIC: What?

KELLY: (INTIMATELY.) Well, you're grabbing me round the waist.

ERIC: Jeez! Sorry!

KELLY: No! I *like* it. It's kind of . . . masterful?

ERIC: You think so?

KELLY: What's happening to your hair line? It's rolling back like a sardine tin!

ERIC: Oh . . . Yeah . . . it does that when the girl of my dreams spills tea all over me.

KELLY: Girl of your dreams?

ERIC: Did I say that? Cripes! Let's swing it, Baby!

DANCE MUSIC SWELLS AND DANCING FEET ARE HEARD.

KELLY: Wicked!

CORNELIA: Wicked is right! I think you've done it, Cornelia. I really think you've *done* it. Roll on the pretzel maker!

SHORT INTERLUDE OF DANCE MUSIC AS TIME MOVES ALONG.

SCENE TWO

ERIC: This is fantastic, Kelly.

KELLY: I know! I've never had such a great time! You are one terrific dancer, Eric.

ERIC: You think so?

KELLY: It's swell to be with a good dancer. Those guys that step all over you! This is a real treat.

ERIC: It's the feet, you see. You have to have the right feet.

TAPPING TOES AS HE DEMONSTRATES HIS SKILL. TAPPITY-TAP TAP-TAP, TAP TAP TAP.

KELLY: Wow! Definitely!

ERIC: Wanna go round one more time?

KELLY: Are you kidding? I'm worn out!

ERIC: You are? But we've only been dancing thirty minutes.

KELLY: Thirty minutes? Oh my lord! Rocky! I forgot all about him.

ERIC: Rocky?

KELLY: My date. I'm actually here with another guy. It was his tea I spilled all over you.

ERIC: Yeah well, you're with me now. It's predestined.

KELLY: Oh, you say such cute things. *Predestined.*

ERIC: It means that we're meant to be together, and nothing can separate us.

KELLY: Well, I think Rocky could. He's kind of a . . . heavyweight. You know what I mean?

ERIC: Hey! Leave Rocky to me.

KELLY: Really?

ERIC: No problem. I can handle him. Look, you sure you don't want to dance some more?

KELLY: I can't! I need a break. Powder my nose. You know.

ERIC: Well maybe we could have some tea.

KELLY: (MOVING OFF.) That would be swell.

ERIC: Darjeeling or Earl Grey?

KELLY: What? Oh. Earl Grey.

ERIC: You know where my table is.

KELLY: (FROM AFAR.) Yeah, I'll just be a second.

SCENE THREE

LAID BACK MUSIC. ERIC SITS DOWN.

CORNELIA: Pretty nimble on your feet for a wall flower.

ERIC: Was I OK?

CORNELIA: Fred would have been proud.

ERIC: One look at Kelly and something came over me. I couldn't help myself.

CORNELIA: It was Ballroom at first sight.

ERIC: I turned cold and then hot. I couldn't resist the impulse.

CORNELIA: Where is she, anyway?

ERIC: Powdering her nose. I have to order more tea.

CORNELIA: I ordered you fresh, with sandwiches and cakes. So, you're having a good time?

ERIC: I'm having a *spectacular* time. I don't know how to thank you. Should I be paying a fee for this?

CORNELIA: Heavens no. I'm taking enough chances as it is. They'd take away my licence if I charged you too.

ERIC: Who would? Look, who *did* send you here?

CORNELIA: I can't tell you.

ERIC: Come on, who?

CORNELIA: I *can* say it wasn't your mother.

CRASH AS ROCKY LURCHES AGAINST THE TABLE.

CORNELIA: Well, *hello* there.

ERIC: Watch it!

ROCKY: No. You watch it buddy. I've gotta bone to pick with you.

CORNELIA: Oh! Pick it with *me,* lover boy!

ROCKY: Where do you get off, dancing with my girl?

ERIC: Kelly's . . . *your* girl?

ROCKY: Yeah. And I'm mad as hell. And when I'm mad, I feel like taking things apart. You get me?

ERIC: Well, I didn't know she was your girl.

ROCKY: She didn't mention me?

ERIC: Why should she? Look, I'm not into the male territorial thing. I'm only here for the tea. OK?

CORNELIA: That's not what you said before.

ERIC: Cornelia!

ROCKY: What did he say before?

CORNELIA: (SUGGESTIVELY.) That she made him turn all hot and cold.

ERIC: Cornelia! Look I didn't know Kelly was spoken for. She's all yours.

ROCKY: Yeah well, she'd better be. 'Cos if I catch her with you again, you wanna know what I'll do?

ERIC: No.

ROCKY: See this chair?

ERIC: Yes.

ROCKY: Describe it to me.

ERIC: Well, uh, it's a standard hotel chair. Simple but sturdy, metal frame, wooden fretwork. Plush seats. Ohhh!

EXCRUCIATING SOUNDS OF METAL AND WOOD CRUNCHING AND BENDING.

ROCKY: *There*. Now what does it look like?

ERIC: (SCARED OUT OF HIS POTATO.) Like a pretzel?

ROCKY: You got it. They don't call me the Pretzel Maker for nothing. (MOVING OFF.) So hands off, right?

ERIC: Like I said, I'm here for the tea? . . . Brother!

CORNELIA: Woo-ee! What a centre fold!

ERIC: You think he's good looking?

CORNELIA: Totally carnal. Oh boy, you're really sweating.

ERIC: Its hot in here. *Fff*. My brow is soaking!

CORNELIA: Here, have a napkin.

ERIC: Thanks. Hey. My hairline's still rolled back. When'll it go back to normal?

CORNELIA: Hard to say.

ERIC: You mean I could be stuck with this?

CORNELIA: Listen Sunshine, your hairline's the least of your problems. What are you going to do when Kelly gets back?

ERIC: You're the soothsayer. You tell me.

CORNELIA: Well, it's doesn't take a Rhodes Scholar to see that Rocky's going to make bow ties out of you if you dance with her again.

ERIC: Yeah well, he can't make anything out of me if I'm not here.

ERIC'S CHAIR SCRAPING.

CORNELIA: You tried that before. It won't work. And anyway, how can you be such a chicken!

ERIC: Chickening out is the better part of valour. Besides, my hairline's back to normal.

KELLY: Hi Eric.

ERIC: Kelly! Oh my god! Look uh Kelly . . . I hate to dance and run but you . . . like . . . Holy Crumoly!

CORNELIA: There goes the hairline again.

ERIC: (MAKES STRANGE NOISES OF METAMORPHOSIS.) Oomph. Werfff!

KELLY: I love it when you look at me like that.

ERIC: And do you like it when I hold you like this?

KELLY: Ahh! Yes!

ERIC: Well then. Let's go for it!

KELLY: Wicked!

ROCKY: (RETURNING.) Hey! That joker's dancing with Kelly again.

CORNELIA: Have a seat, big boy.

ROCKY: Is he out of his mind? Doesn't he know what I'll do to him? Hey! Hey I warned you! Come back here!

CORNELIA: Rocky! (SIGH.) I thought this would be easy.

SCENE FOUR

ERIC AND KELLY OUT OF BREATH.

KELLY: Sooner or later he's going to catch us, you know.

ERIC: Yeah, but until he does, I'm in heaven.

KELLY: You dancing fool!

ERIC: Are you tired?

KELLY: Not anymore. I could do this forever.

ERIC: Me too.

KELLY: Oh, I love it when you hold me close like this. You sure are a passionate dancer.

ERIC: Passion's my middle name.

KELLY: When you danced me across the tabletops. Wow! It was like being on the silver screen. Like an old movie.

ERIC: It was the only way to give Rocky the slip. He could keep up with us on the floor but not on the tables. The poor guy has no sense of balance.

KELLY: Whereas you could probably do this on a tight rope.

ERIC: It's all your doing, you know. Until I met you, I was a klutz. A real bumblefoot. My toes were all thumbs.

KELLY: I find that hard to believe.

ERIC: I thought I was destined to spend the rest of my life as a wallflower.

KELLY: Oh, go on!

ERIC: Really. This is my fourth tea dance. The other three times I hid behind my teacup, wishing I could get up the courage to ask someone to dance.

KELLY: But you're a *terrific* dancer!

ERIC: Well yeah. With you. You know what they say about hearing the earth shake? Well, it's true. From the first minute I saw you the earth's been jazzing and jitterbugging under my feet. The only way I can cope with it is to dance along.

KELLY: I love the things you say.

ERIC: Well, I gotta couple of other things I want to say too.

KELLY: You do?

ERIC: Yeah, while I still have the nerve. Why don't we just go behind this pillar here.

KELLY: Okay.

ERIC: So, um . . . Do you like cats?

DANCE MUSIC SWELLS UP.

SCENE FIVE

CORNELIA: Did they give you the slip?

ROCKY: Yeah. I'll say one thing for that Bozo. He sure is fast on his feet. I've been chasing them for over half an hour.

CORNELIA: You must be exhausted. Have some tea.

ROCKY: Thanks. (SLURPS AND CHOKES.) What *is* this.

CORNELIA: It's Earl Grey.

ROCKY: Am I supposed to drink it or dab it behind my ears?

CORNELIA: All that muscle and witty too. So, tell me, how did you get to be so . . . *rugged.*

ROCKY: Hey, it wasn't easy, you know.

CORNELIA: I'll bet. You must've worn out a whole fleet of Nautiluses.

ROCKY: And for what. To get thrown over for that rabbit-faced pipsqueak.

CORNELIA: Hey, don't take it so bad. There's lots of other turkeys in the straw.

ROCKY: Uh . . . What exactly is your role in all this?

CORNELIA: I'm a wish therapist.

ROCKY: Wish therapist?

CORNELIA: It means that I can make your wishes come true. But—and this is the kick—I can also change what you wish for. Why don't I read your teacup?

ROCKY: I dunno. I don't go in for that extra sensory junk.

CORNELIA: What's wrong with *extra* sensory?

ROCKY: Uh. Well, if you put it that way. Uhm, don't you need my cup?

CUP SCRITCHING.

CORNELIA: Oh yes. Silly me. Now, let's see. Yes, lots of leaves in there. So. I'll turn your cup three times in a clockwise direction . . . and . . . ah yes. Hmhm.

DANCE MUSIC.

ROCKY: Hey! There they are!

ROCKY RISING NOISILY.

CORNELIA: Where?

ROCKY: I can see them. Halfway behind that pillar over there.

CORNELIA: I don't think that's them.

ROCKY: I'd know that balding brow anywhere! (MOVING OFF.) I'll fix him.

CORNELIA: Now wait. Don't be too hasty. Rocky! Hold on. Rats!

DANCE MUSIC TAKES OVER.

SCENE SIX

ERIC: You mean you will?

KELLY: Yes, yes, yes, yes, yes!

ERIC: I don't believe it. This is fantastic.

JAUNTY LITTLE TAP DANCE RHYTHM TAPPITY-TAP TAP-TAP, TAP TAP TAP.

ERIC: You realize you're totally out of your mind. You've known me for less than two hours and you're saying yes!!! Daddly-da dah dah, dah dah dah!

ANOTHER JAUNTY LITTLE TAP DANCE—TAPPITY-TAP TAP-TAP, TAP TAP TAP.

KELLY: Of course, I'm saying yes. You can't fight predestination. Will you teach me how to do that?

ERIC: Sure. Just put your feet like this. Dah Dah.

TAP TAP.

KELLY: Like this? Dah Dah.

TAP TAP.

ERIC: Then like this. Daddly dah dah.

TAPPITY TAP TAP.

KELLY: Daddly dah dah.

TAPPITY TAP TAP.

ERIC: Then let your feet take it.

TAPPITY-TAP TAP-TAP, TAP TAP TAP.

KELLY: Let your feet take it.

TAPPITY-TAP TAP-TAP, TAP TAP TAP.

ERIC: You got it! What a team.

ROCKY: (SNARL OF A MAN IN A WHITE RAGE.)

KELLY: Rocky!

ERIC: Uh, Hi Rock!

ROCKY: I don't believe I'm seeing this. My best girl dancing with a rabbit! Well, you've danced yourself into a corner, Chump!

ERIC: Now hold on a minute.

ROCKY: *You* hold on. Hold on to everything you got because I'm going to take you apart limb by limb.

KELLY: Rocky! Don't hurt him!

ROCKY: Nobody messes with the *Pretzel Maker.*

CHASE SCENE. TABLES OVERTURNING. DISHES BREAKING. ERIC YELLING OUT LIKE STAN LAUREL. ROCKY ROARING WITH RAGE. ENDS WITH CRY FROM ERIC AND DOORS SLAMMING.

SCENE SEVEN

KELLY: I should have followed them. I should have gone outside. But I couldn't bear to see it! Oh Cornelia, what am I going to do?

CORNELIA: Now Kelly, calm down! Eric can take care of himself.

KELLY: But they've been out there for ages!

CORNELIA: He'll be all right.

KELLY: You don't know Rocky. He's a killing machine. Do you know what they call him at the gym? The *Pretzel* Maker!

CORNELIA: It's just a metaphor, ok?

KELLY: A metaphor for *murder!*

CORNELIA: Oh . . . here he *comes*!

KELLY: Eric? Thank God!

CORNELIA: No, *Rocky!* Man is he built!

ROCKY: (MARCHES BACK GRUNTING AND MUTTERING WITH SATISFACTION.) Guess I fixed him.

KELLY: Rocky! What did you do to him?

ROCKY: You can scratch his name from your list of admirers.

KELLY: Admirers! He's my fiancé, you big boob!

ROCKY: How can he be your fiancé? You haven't known him for more than an hour.

KELLY: One hour and thirty-seven minutes!

ROCKY: I don't get it. I thought you and me . . . that we . . .

KELLY: He's the only one I've ever loved!

ROCKY: The only one! But what about me?

KELLY: You? You murderer! I hope I never see you again!

ROCKY: But why? What's he got that I haven't got?

KELLY: Well in the first place he's got cats. Three of them. You never liked my cats!

ROCKY: They make me sneeze. Aw come on Kelly. How could you love that scrawny little ferret? I bet he doesn't weigh 140 pounds.

KELLY: That's all you ever think about, working out.

ROCKY: But you're the reason I worked out in the first place.

KELLY: Oh, what am I going to do, Cornelia? I'm never going to see him again.

CORNELIA: Don't give up hope. I read his teacup, you know.

KELLY: Eric's cup? Was I in it?

CORNELIA: Yeah. You were pretty prominent at the beginning.

KELLY: And then?

CORNELIA: It got a little murky. It had a horse, though.

KELLY: A horse? What's a horse got to do with anything?

ROCKY: Horses make me sneeze.

KELLY: Ohhhh! He said it was predestination. That nothing could ever separate us.

ROCKY: Yeah well, he didn't reckon on . . . the Pretzel Maker!

KELLY: Oh, dry up! You've ruined my *life*. I never want to see you again!

ROCKY: Never? But Kelly!

DOORS BURSTING OPEN.

ROCKY: What's that?

CORNELIA: There seems to be some commotion over there.

KELLY: The doors just burst open.

ROCKY: What's all the fuss about?

KELLY: It's Eric . . . He's on a *horse*.

CORNELIA: Really? Maybe I went a little too far this time.

WHINNY!

KELLY: He's headed this way.

HOOFBEATS GALLOPING THROUGH THE ROOM, CRIES OF AWE.

ROCKY: He's gonna trample us. Ahh!

KELLY: Na, he's just going to sweep me off my feet. Over here, Eric!

ERIC: Hang on, Kelly. I'm coming!

GALLOPING CLOSER AND CLOSER. WHINNY.

KELLY: Eric!

ERIC: Here! Grab my hand!

SWOOSH AND CRIES OF DELIGHT AS KELLY IS SWEPT UP ONTO THE HORSE. THEN HORSE GALLOPING OFF.

ERIC: (MOVING OFF.) Thanks Cornelia!

KELLY: Goodbye!

DOORS SLAMMING.

ROCKY: *Jeez* I'm depressed! How could she fall for a little bald guy like that? I mean look at *my* hair, thick, luxuriant. People would die for hair like this.

CORNELIA: I know *I* would. Let me run my fingers through it. Ooohh

ROCKY: And do you know how long I've been working out? Look at that bicep. I mean you don't see biceps like that every day.

CORNELIA: Hmm. Your pecs are pretty good too.

ROCKY: I turned myself from a 98 lb. weakling into a major hunk just for her. What am I going to do now? . . . Say! What about this wish therapy? You think you can do anything for me?

CORNELIA: Well, I still have your cup here. Let me have a look.

ROCKY: What do you see, suicide?

CORNELIA: I see . . . a ship. You're on a ship.

ROCKY: Are you sure? I get seasick.

CORNELIA: (LOSING PATIENCE A LITTLE.) So, take Gravol. It's like a romantic cruise, ok? . . . I see a woman.

ROCKY: Tell me more.

CORNELIA: Very dark, very tall.

ROCKY: Dark and tall is good.

CORNELIA: Spiky red heels.

ROCKY: Really. Hey . . . You've got spiky red heels.

CORNELIA: Black leather. Fishnet stockings . . .

ROCKY: So, let me get this straight. You re-arranged the tea leaves?

CORNELIA: Uh huh.

ROCKY: Messed up my head. Made me wish for something or should I say some*one* different.

CORNELIA: You're gonna report me, aren't you.

ROCKY: Well, there are some things you could never make me want.

CORNELIA: (IN A RUSH.) This is the first time I've used my powers to my own advantage. I swear! It's just that the minute I laid my eyes on you tonight, pushy and brassy and built like a Mack Truck, I knew I had to get my hands on your . . . teacup.

ROCKY: You can push my tea leaves around till the cows come home but there are some things you're never gonna get me to do. Like you'll *never* get me on a ship. Right?

CORNELIA: Right.

ROCKY: So . . . could you maybe take out the ship and put in a Harley Davidson?

CORNELIA: Well yeah . . . No sweat.

ROCKY: But keep the fishnets, Okay?

CORNELIA: OKAY!!!

DANCE MUSIC SWELLS DRAMATICALLY AND THEN GRADUALLY FADES OUT.

LOVE AND WAR WESTERN STYLE

Love and War Western Style was commissioned by Morningside, CBC. It aired in April, 1991 in 5 daily episodes. Series Producer was James Roy.

Produced and Directed by	MARTIE FISHMAN
Recording Engineer	ROBERT DOBLE
Sound Effects Technician	UTE SCHAFFLAND
Production Assistant	CHRISTINE STOREY
Composer/Keyboards	MILES JACKSON

CAST:

Betty Cooper	MOTHER (ELDER)
Marie Hohtanz	VINNIE/NARRATOR
Wally McSweem	DAD (ELDER)
James Dugan	UNCLE DONALD (ELDER)
Barbara Campbell-Brown	BERYL (ELDER)
Karen Planden	VINNIE
Joyce Doolittle	MOTHER
Kevin Cork	ANDY
Katherine Venour	BERYL
Robert Benson	DAD
Hal Kerbes	UNCLE DONALD
Stephen Sparks	CLYDE
Rodney Padmos	PARNELL
Grant Lowe	GIL
Judith Buchan	HALLIE
Daryl Shuttleworth	BOGGS
Linda Kupecek	NAOMI
Brenda Pennock	NORA
Rose Scollard	HALLIE (ELDER)

CAST OF CHARACTERS

The course of true love in the west is a bumpy ride according to *Vinnie Randall,* and to prove it you need go no further than her father *Leo*'s overriding love for her mother *Nellie*, her sister *Beryl*'s sparring-match-made-in-heaven with *Clyde*, and her *Uncle Donald*'s perilous and wacky pursuit of *Hallie Bedford.*

Complicit in these stories and invariably muddying and diverting the plot lines are brother *Andy*, the sleazy but dishy *Parnell Lang*, the magnanimous bestower of peas *Naomi Prince*, and the devious and scheming *Nora Tamprey.*

Gil Cobbett, the *Conductor*, and *Jeff Boggs* are completely innocent bystanders.

EPISODE ONE

SCENE ONE

"WHEN YOU WORE A TULIP" SUNG RIOTOUSLY BY THE RANDALL FAMILY, GATHERED AROUND THE PIANO. THE SONG FADES INTO THE NARRATION.

VINNIE/NARRATOR: "When You Wore a Tulip." Now there's a song that takes you back. We sang it all the time in the forties.

LEO: (FROM THE PIANO.) It goes back a lot farther than that, Vinnie.

VINNIE/NARR: I know, Dad. But it's the forties it makes me think of. I would have to say the forties after the war was the best time of our lives. Don't know if I can pin down why exactly.

NELLIE: (FROM PIANO.) It was the post war mood, dear.

VINNIE/NARR: True. But it was more than that. It seems, looking back, that there was a timeless quality to everything. Alberta in those days was a place of high hopes and high jinks. And Thigh Bone, my hometown, was as golden and fragrant and as steeped in romance as a three-volume novel.

LEO: Romance? In Thigh Bone? Hogwash!

VINNIE/NARR: Well for sure you wouldn't find a Lorna Doone or a Jane Eyre.

LEO: You sure wouldn't. Around here a woman had to be lassooed, thrown and tied before a man would dare propose to them.

THE FAMILY LAUNCHES INTO "AIN'T SHE SWEET."

VINNIE/NARR: All the same, I would put the amorous ordeals of the women of Thigh Bone right up there with the best of them. Take my mother.

LEO: (FROM PIANO.) I did!

ALL: (GENERAL PROTEST.) Dad! Leo! Eugh!

VINNIE/NARR: If you asked her, my mother would tell you her marriage to Dad was made in heaven.

NELLIE: Oh yes, Dear. Your father was a very romantic man.

VINNIE/NARR: See what I mean?

NELLIE: Oh yes. I was head over heels.

UNCLE DONALD: Well, *that's* true. Head over heels!

NELLIE: Now Donald.

VINNIE/NARR: Head over heels was an unfortunate choice of words. Mother may have been in seventh heaven with Dad but for most of her married life she'd had to endure one serious flaw in her paradise. And that was Dad's nasty habit of running her over.

LEO: Nasty habit! What kind of talk is that? You'd think I was some kind of loose character.

UNCLE DONALD: Let's see now, Nellie. How many times is it that you've flipped over Leo?

NELLIE: There's no need to get silly, Donald.

UNCLE DONALD: There was the surrey when he was courting you. And the bull team. The very first time he got them he . . .

NELLIE: Donald! That's enough!

VINNIE/NARR: Donald was right, though. Every farm animal Dad ever drove, the bull team, the Clydesdales, the neighbour's mares, sooner or later he drove them over Mother.

SCENE TWO

FARAWAY SOUNDS OF BULL TEAM AND DAD SOOTHING THEM.

VINNIE/NARR: I must have been about three years old at the time. Dad was in the yard, unhitching the bulls from the plough, when Mother came out of the root cellar with a can of cream she'd been cooling down there.

LEO: It was her apron flapping that set them off. Or a heel fly. Something startled them.

GALLOPING HOOVES AND DAD SHOUTING. CRASH! CONFUSION AND NELLIE'S CRIES!

VINNIE/NARR: Whatever it was, Dan and McGoo chose that moment to bolt. They headed right for Mother, with Dad tangled up in the traces galloping noisily behind. Mother was trampled by all three, but mostly by Dad.

LEO: She was basically unharmed, right? I mean the plough could've still been hitched to them and that would've been a *real* disaster. She was lucky.

ALL: (UNBELIEVINGLY.) Lucky?!

VINNIE/NARR: The real nightmare for Mother began when Dad entered the mechanized era. At the time I'm speaking of Mother would have been about 37, 38. She was in good shape for her age.

NELLIE: I liked to keep trim.

LEO: Your mother was always a looker. She had great legs.

UNCLE DONALD: And you know why. She got them from hopping out of your way all those years.

VINNIE/NARR: Mother could turn heads when she came into a room. She made her own clothes but there was always a bit of style to them. And her hats, she made those too, from straw forms and baubles she ordered from Eaton's. I remember . . . (FADES OUT.)

SCENE THREE

RADIO FAINTLY PLAYING "PEG OF MY HEART."

VINNIE: This is the best hat you've ever done, Mum.

NELLIE: You think so? I am rather pleased with it.

BERYL: Put it on . . . Yeah. It's great. What do you think, Andy? Isn't it lovely?

ANDY: I guess. How come it's got all those cherries on it?

VINNIE: The cherries are the whole point, Dimwit.

CHINKING OF COOKIE JAR.

BERYL: And stay out of the cookies.

CLUNK OF JAR CLOSING SUDDENLY.

ANDY: You're not my boss. AW!

NELLIE: Now children, if I've told you . . .

SHE IS DROWNED OUT BY THE RATTLING AND CRANKING OF AN OLD TRUCK—COUGHING, SPITTING, BACKFIRING.

VINNIE: It's Dad. He's driving a truck.

ANDY: That's Art Swainson's truck. It's a real rattletrap.

BERYL: A death trap, you mean.

EVERYONE SHOUTS IN TERROR. TRUCK BRAKING TO A HALT! SIGHS OF RELIEF.

BERYL: For a minute there I didn't think he was going to stop.

NELLIE: I didn't know your father could drive.

BERYL: (UNDER HER BREATH.) He can't!

DAD ENTERS.

LEO: Well now, kids, Nellie. Nellie? What's that on your head?

NELLIE: Oh, I'm just trying something out, Leo.

LEO: Looks like a reject from a bake sale. What's for lunch? I'm starving!

NELLIE: (STIFFLY.) Cheese sandwiches.

MOTHER PACING ABOUT, SLAMMING DOORS AND DISHES.

LEO: I have to drive all the way to Stettler and get that load of ties I bought, last week. Cheese isn't going to get me to Stettler and back, Nellie.

ANDY: Can I go with you, Dad?

VINNIE: Me too?

LEO: I thought your mother might want to come along. Do a little shopping while we're there.

NELLIE: I have things to do.

LEO: Like what?

NELLIE: Like going over to the west quarter this afternoon and getting the sweep.

LEO: That won't take all day, Nellie.

NELLIE: I have ironing to do, supper to cook.

LEO: Well, no one's forcing you. So, what about lunch.

NELLIE: Cheese is right there in the icebox, Leo. Bread's in the bread bin.

LEO: Maybe I'll get something in Stettler.

SCENE FOUR

VINNIE/NARR: Andy and I went off to Stettler with Dad. Beryl stayed behind to help Mother with the ironing and the supper. It wasn't until late afternoon that Mother got around to getting the sweep. Like most farm wives, my mother did her share of the field work and enjoyed it too.

NELLIE: I really loved driving that hay sweep!

LEO: Nellie knew how to handle a sweep, all right. Better at it than any hired hand. And that's no lie.

SCENE FIVE

NELLIE: Here Heathcliff. Come on old boy.

WHINNY AND HOOVES.

NELLIE: Atta boy. Such a nice horse. Uh-uh! No sugar till we get this bridle on you.

VINNIE/NARR: Anything Mother did outside—haying, seeding, washing—she wore a hat. Since she wasn't actually going to be working, she wore her new hat that day. The one with the cherries.

WHINNY AND HOOVES THROUGH NEXT TWO SPEECHES.

VINNIE/NARR: After she caught Heathcliff, she rode him over to the west section and hitched him up to the sweep.

NELLIE: Easy boy. Let me strap you into this. There we go. Now I'll just get up here and . . . Off we go! (SINGS.) "When you wore a tulip, a bright yellow tulip, and I wore a big red rose." (SONG FADES OFF.)

CLOP-CLOP AND SINGING IN THE BACKGROUND.

VINNIE/NARR: To get from the west to the east quarter section of our farm you had to take the road so you could cross Thigh Bone Creek. Mother was halfway down the steeply banked road to the bridge when Heathcliff started to act up.

WHINNY AND SNORT.

NELLIE: Whoa boy! Steady now. Steady!

RATTLE TRAP SOUNDS FROM AFAR.

VINNIE/NARR: Mother looked behind her and saw something coming over the crest of the hill—Dad, Andy, and me returning from Stettler with the load of ties.

NELLIE: What the dickens? Who's that idiot? Eeee-asy boy!

INSIDE THE TRUCK. GURGLING AND SPUTTERING SOUNDS. AS SCENE PROGRESSES ENGINE BECOMES MORE PROMINENT.

ANDY: You're going pretty fast, Dad.

LEO: I know how to drive, Andy.

VINNIE: You're working up quite a speed.

ANDY: You're supposed to gear down when you drive down a hill.

LEO: Don't talk when I'm driving. Hades! Who's that in the road? They're driving like a Sunday funeral!

HONK! HONK!

VINNIE: It's Mother!

HONK! HONK!

LEO: Your mother? She's not going to make it!

VINNIE: Hit the brakes!

ANDY: Gear *down*, DAD!

BUILDING CLIMAX OF CAR, HORSE, AND WILD CONFUSION.

VINNIE/NARR: Mother, fearful at the way Dad was gaining on her, whipped Heathcliff to a gallop in a vain attempt to outrace him to the bridge.

NELLIE: Gee up! Faster! Speed up, you old nag!

LEO: She's not going to make it! She's not going to make it!

VINNIE & ANDY: Brakes, Dad! Brakes!

LEO: Nellie! Get out of the damned road!

VINNIE/NARR: Preferring certain misery to possible death, Mother took his advice. At the last moment she swerved to the side and went full tilt into the creek, losing her dignity, her temper, and her hat.

WHINNY AND SPLASH AND FLOUNDERING IN THE WATER.

NELLIE: Oh! Oh!! Ohhhhh!! . . . My hat!

RUMBLING OF TRUCK AND TIES FALLING OFF.

VINNIE/NARR: Dad made the bridge, but he dumped almost a quarter of his ties into the fast-flowing stream as he rattled across. They floated away as swiftly as Mother's boater. Mother didn't care a pinch about the ties, but she was a long time forgiving father for the hat.

SCENE SIX

KIDS VOICES. EXCITEMENT. HORN HONKING!

VINNIE: I can't believe we're getting a car!

ANDY: A split visor!

BERYL: Plush seats!

VINNIE: Does the canopy work?

ANDY: Of course, Dumbnut!

VINNIE/NARR: In spite of his fiasco with Swainson's truck, Dad decided soon after to get a car. Billy Counter over near Oatcrest had a 1922 Overland for sale and after long discussions on the pros and cons Dad and Mother made up their minds to get it. As was usual in those days the whole family took part in the transaction. While Dad tried to talk Billy down a dollar or two, Mother visited with Mae Counter and we swarmed all over the object of purchase with the Counter brood, marvelling at its split visor, convertible canvas canopy and blaring Klaxon.

SCENE SEVEN

VINNIE/NARR: At last, the deal was completed and off we chugged into the lengthening prairie evening.

CAR STARTING UP, ENGINE SOUNDS AND EXCITED CHATTER.

ANDY: Do the horn, Dad.

GOO-GOO! GOO-GOO!

VINNIE: This is swell!

BERYL: Is this heaven or what!

ANDY: Try out the wipers, Dad, eh?

LEO: I don't know if we have any, Andy.

ANDY: Sure you do. Right there on the dash.

LEO: This thingummy here?

ANDY: Yea, that's it. Try 'em out, eh?

LEO: There's nothing to wipe.

ANDY: Do it anyway, Dad.

WIPERS SWISHING.

ANDY: Now do the horn.

NELLIE: I think we've done the horn enough, Andy.

LEO: Why not humour the lad, Nellie.

GOO-GOO! GOO-GOO!

BERYL: This is divine!

VINNIE/NARR: Back then even the simplest drive was an excursion. The roads were little more than cart tracks and with the canvas down you were part of the prairie, there were no telephone poles, black top or ditches to keep you apart. Fences were more likely to run across the road than beside it. You hopped out, pulled open the wire and hooked it up again before you went on.

It's not hard to remember that first ride. The grass and flowers came right up to the trail and released their fragrance as they were crushed under the wheels. Grouse and curlews flew up in front of us, grumbling and screeching with annoyance,

Beryl and I lounged in the back like homecoming royalty. Andy, squeezed between us on the plush brown seats, was almost sick with joy. He leaned forward shouting questions into Dad's ear. Mother sat beside Dad, as proud as any of us at our initiation into the modern age. We knew we were in the hands of one who was less than a technical genius, but what the heck, he was only going fifteen miles an hour. He was doing okay by our books. Until we were about two or three hundred yards from our gate.

LEO: Uh, Nellie.

NELLIE: Yes, Dear.

LEO: Just hop out and get that gate.

NELLIE: Yes, Dear.

VINNIE/NARR: It was my mother's way that she did what my father asked without question. It was a reflex action. With the car still running she hopped out and ran ahead to the gate. Although he was travelling slowly, with the gate coming rapidly towards him Dad lost his presence of mind. He literally forgot how to stop the car.

LEO: Hurry up, Nellie!

NELLIE: Yes, Dear.

ANDY: The brake, Dad! Use the brake!

BERYL: You're going to hit her!

CAR THUMPING NELLIE AND GOING THROUGH THE GATE.

NELLIE: Ow!

ALL: CRYING OUT.

VINNIE/NARR: She was pretty spry for a mother of three, but she never made it. A few yards short of the gate Mother was flattened by Dad. He also took out the gate and a few unlucky chickens, who happened to be foraging on the other side, and was a quarter mile into the wheat before he finally ground to a halt.

SCENE EIGHT

PARTYING AROUND PIANO.

BERYL: I will never forget that ride.

VINNIE/NARR: It's a miracle you weren't killed, Mom.

LEO: It was the brakes. Billy Counter should've told me they were wonky.

BERYL: You didn't use the brakes, Dad

LEO: Look, are we gonna sing or are we gonna sit here shooting the breeze all evening!

DONALD: Hit it, Andy!

"WHEN YOU WORE A TULIP" RIOTOUS AND JOYFUL GRADUALLY FADING OUT.

EPISODE TWO

SCENE ONE

"WHEN YOU WORE A TULIP" SUNG BY THE RANDALL FAMILY, GATHERED AROUND THE PIANO. THE SONG FADES INTO THE NARRATION.

VINNIE/NARR: If the romantic events I'm describing to you seem a little rough and ready you have to understand that the women of Thigh Bone were an ornery lot. Maybe it had something to do with the frontier spirit. My mother was one example of the species. My sister Beryl was another.

The year she was 18, Beryl had three offers of marriage. There was the minister of our church, Elmer Brady.

BERYL: I'm sorry, Elmer. I don't think I'm ready for such an important stepping stone in my life.

VINNIE/NARR: There was a young homesteader from North Dakota named Billy Schultz.

BERYL: Billy. You're a wonderful person, but I'm not ready to tie the knot. You know?

VINNIE/NARR: And there was Clyde Fenstrom.

BERYL: Get lost, Clyde.

SCENE TWO

TINKERING ON THE OVERLAND'S STARTER.

LEO: Three proposals! Beryl's had three offers of marriage? Pull the other one, Donald.

UNCLE DONALD: Cross my heart, Leo. Reverend Brady. Billy Schultz. And Clyde.

LEO: Well, it'll be Clyde, won't it. Beryl and Clyde, the old sparring partners.

APPROACHING FOOTSTEPS IN GRAVEL.

UNCLE DONALD: The boxing match made in heaven. Hi Nellie.

NELLIE: I came out to see if you want some tea.

LEO: Sure do. The starter on this thing's got the better of us . . . So. Beryl said yes to Clyde?

NELLIE: Apparently not.

LEO: I don't believe it. A girl who looks like Beryl should snap up the first offer she gets.

NELLIE: Now, Leo.

LEO: Nellie, you know as well as I do that Beryl can't hope to get by on looks.

NELLIE: Leo!

LEO: It's true. Even as baby she was plug ugly. Remember what Donald here said when she was born?

NELLIE: How can we forget. You've been repeating it once a month for the past eighteen years.

LEO: Your own brother here said she looked more like a bull terrier than a baby.

NELLIE: He was only five years old, Leo.

LEO: Out of the mouths of babes.

UNCLE DONALD: I have said profounder things in the years since, Leo. And wittier.

LEO: What's she gonna do if she doesn't get married?

NELLIE: She's going to raise chickens.

LEO: Chickens? She's nuts!

NELLIE: She's just out of High School, Leo. She's not ready to give up her independence.

LEO: Nuts.

NELLIE: (STIFFLY.) I'll go make the tea.

LEO: So, let's see how she starts now.

GRINDING OF STARTER.

UNCLE DONALD: Shouldn't you get in the car first, Leo?

GRINDING CONTINUES AND ENGINE KICKS IN.

UNCLE DONALD: Leo! Get in the car . . .

LEO: I am! I am!

UNCLE DONALD: Nellie! Run for it.

CAR CAREENING TOWARDS NELLIE. HER DISTANT CRIES.

SCENE THREE

CLINKING CUP.

BERYL: Here Mum, drink this. It's good and hot and I put lots of sugar in it.

UNCLE DONALD: You nearly did for her this time, Leo.

LEO: I stopped it in time, didn't I?

BERYL: Barely.

NELLIE: This is the fifth time this has happened, Leo.

LEO: But look, Nellie. The good thing about the Overland is it's set really high, right?

NELLIE: (DUBIOUSLY.) Yes.

LEO: So. As long as you remember to keep your head down when it's rolling over you, you're not in that much danger.

ALL: Leo! Dad!

SCENE FOUR

BERYL: The chicken was once a jungle fowl, domesticated in Southwest Asia 3,000 years ago . . .

BERYL: . . . over 100 varieties, including egg, meat, and dual-purpose breeds . . .

BERYL: . . . then the interest on 230 dollars at 3 percent over two and a half years would be . . .

VINNIE/NARR: Having spurned her three suitors, Beryl got on with her career plans. She sent away for every feed company and government brochure available and sat up nights, plotting and replotting ways to stretch her meagre bank account. Deciding that a hundred chickens would be a good number to start with, she asked Uncle Donald to help her build a coop.

UNCLE DONALD: Why sure, Kid. But it doesn't need to be for a hundred. Half of them are bound to die before they reach laying age.

BERYL: You do realize we're in the twentieth century, Uncle Donald.

UNCLE DONALD: Well. I'd heard something to that effect.

BERYL: And have you heard of scientific method?

UNCLE DONALD: I have an inkling.

BERYL: Let me tell you about chickens, Uncle Donald. Let me tell you about the advances that have been made since the dark ages that you were evidently raised in.

UNCLE DONALD: I'm only five years older than you, Beryl.

VINNIE/NARR: After a brisk diatribe from Beryl scathingly introducing him to the Twentieth Century and Scientific Method, Donald agreed to build for a hundred.

SCENE FIVE

HAMMERING AND SAWING BEGINS AND CONTINUES UNDER THE FOLLOWING:

UNCLE DONALD: Help me with this beam.

BERYL: How's this?

UNCLE DONALD: That's it! Now hold it steady.

VINNIE/NARR: When they realized Beryl was serious in her refusals, two thirds of her suitors dropped away. The Reverend Brady married Minty Bradshaw, the town's librarian, and Billy Schultz paired off with Amy Pemberton, a buxom, fresh-faced girl from Berryvale.

Clyde did not drop away. What's more, he took an avid interest in Beryl's project. He was there through the entire construction of the chicken coop.

CLYDE: It's nice to see you two doing some honest work for a change.

BERYL: What are you doing here, Clyde?

UNCLE DONALD: Hey pal. So. What do you think?

CLYDE: Hmm. That cross beam's a little off-centre, Donald.

UNCLE DONALD: Really? I checked it three times.

CLYDE: Looks out of kilter to me.

VINNIE/NARR: If you look at the pictures of those days, Clyde Fenstrom turns up in more than a few of them, wickedly handsome, grinning widely, as though he's just pulled off another of his practical jokes. Girls loved him, mothers mistrusted him. Not our mother though. Mum had a real soft spot for Clyde.

NELLIE: (CALLING FROM THE PORCH.) Clyde. So lovely to see you. I bet you'd like a nice cold glass of lemonade.

CLYDE: I sure would Mrs. Randall. Your lemonade is something to write home about.

NELLIE: It's my grandmother's recipe.

BERYL: You're such a suck, Clyde.

VINNIE/NARR: While Beryl and Donald toiled in the hot sun, Clyde lolled in the shade of the poplars, downing glass after glass of Mother's lemonade, occasionally calling out a word or two of advice.

CLYDE: Aren't you going to sand those perches?

UNCLE DONALD: What the heck for?

CLYDE: Chickens are no different to anyone else, Donald. They like their comfort. And I hope you're putting screens at the window. If you don't give them lots of air, they could smother.

UNCLE DONALD: If you're so smart why aren't you building this?

CLYDE: Hey, I leave that kind of work to the experts.

SCENE SIX

VINNIE/NARR: It took a week for the coop to be finished to Beryl's satisfaction. She put up the fence around their yard herself. Dad installed the brooder lamp and drove her to the hatchery to pick up her nine dozen chicks. Clyde was there when they brought the chickens home. When Beryl gave him the grand tour of her operation, he smiled gently and assured her he would be there when it all fell through.

NINE DOZEN CHICKS PEEPING AND SCRATCHING.

CLYDE: Really. When the last chicken quits, I'll put you out of your misery and marry you.

BERYL: Planning on being a bachelor, are you?

CLYDE: Not for long. A couple of months. No. I'll be fair and give it a year.

BERYL: You'll give *what* a year?

CLYDE: This chicken raising nonsense. I say by the end of a year of hustling feed and burying the dead, you'll be ready to call it quits.

BERYL: Quits! Not so long as there's a chicken in that pen!

CLYDE: Like I said, a year. If there's a single bird in that pen by the end of next July, just one, I'll give up on you. I'll tie up with someone else, Nora Tamprey or Cynthia Searles, or someone, and leave you to your independence. Just one chicken.

BERYL: One! There'll be dozens! Hundreds!

VINNIE/NARR: As Dad likes to say, the Gods come down heavy on a proud talker. For a while though, it looked as if Beryl's boast had escaped Divine notice and the chickens flourished as she'd predicted.

It was somewhere in the middle of October that things began to go amiss.

SCENE SEVEN

TINKERING WITH CAR. CHICKENS PROTESTING IN DISTANCE.

ANDY: What's with Beryl, Dad? She's been in the chicken pen for the last half hour.

LEO: Picking up chickens, you mean? Damn this thing!

ANDY: Try loosening that little gismo.

SQUAWK!

ANDY: Look! She's doing it again. She's picked up more than forty chickens in the past hour.

LEO: She's been doing it all day. Looking at the undersides of chickens, frowning and shaking her head. She's going round the bend, Andy.

ANDY: Is there something wrong with the chickens?

LEO: I figure it's lack of male companionship. Someone should give Clyde a call. Who's that?

PICKUP PULLING INTO THE YARD.

ANDY: It's Gil Cobbett. He's the supervisor over at the hatchery.

LEO: What the . . . ? Now *he's* looking at chicken bellies. Maybe he's going round the bend too.

ANDY: Boy. Does she look mad!

SCENE EIGHT

BERYL: Do you see what I mean?

CHICKENS MUTTERING.

BERYL: Cockerels, Mr. Cobbett. All cockerels! There isn't a pullet among them!

GIL: Sure beats me how that many got by us.

BERYL: I have the receipt right here.

RUSTLING PAPER.

BERYL: Here we are. This receipt signed by your own hand says you sold me nine dozen pullets.

GIL: Beats me how that many got by us.

BERYL: You're going to replace them, I trust. I can't run an egg business with a hundred *roosters*.

GIL: We'll replace them, of course. But it sure beats me how that many got by us.

SCENE NINE

VINNIE/NARR: The next day Gil Cobbett's assistant drove out with the replacements and took away the cockerels. He was grinning insanely the whole time. Mother thought she recognized him and mentioned him at supper.

SUPPER SOUNDS.

NELLIE: That hatchery boy, Leo? I'm sure I saw him in town Saturday. With Clyde.

ANDY: They're on the same horseshoe team.

BERYL: I knew it! I knew it wasn't an accident!

LEO: You think Clyde had something to do with your pullets being roosters?

BERYL: Do I ever!

SCENE TEN

BERYL: Let's see . . . If each chicken lays once every two days, I should get . . . No, I'll make it every three days. Then I'll get . . .

BERYL: Candling is a simple operation by which . . .

VINNIE/NARR: With the second batch of chickens safely in her pen, Beryl began counting her eggs. She made endless lists of things she meant to do with her money, mostly boring items that had to do with the egg business. When the rest of us went to a show or a party, Beryl stayed home to read books on candling or chicken diseases.

It was about the second week of January that the disappearances started.

SCENE ELEVEN

KITCHEN SCREEN DOOR OPENING AND SLAMMING SHUT.

BERYL: I'll kill him. I'll *kill* him!

LEO: What's up?

BERYL: There are only ninety birds in the pen!

LEO: Something must've got in at them.

BERYL: Something on two legs. There's no sign of a struggle.

VINNIE/NARR: That night we slept with the bedroom window open so we could hear any ruckus that might start up in the chicken coop. By the end of the week no ruckus had been heard but another seven chickens were gone.

SCENE TWELVE

BERYL: It's Clyde.

LEO: I'm not buying that. I don't see how anyone can steal a chicken without putting the whole damn coop in an uproar.

ANDY: I can.

BERYL: So, tell us, you disgusting little know-it-all.

ANDY: I will. For a price.

BERYL: Forget it.

SCENE THIRTEEN

VINNIE/NARR: A week and six chickens later Beryl was ready to hand over the dollar Andy was asking. That night she sat up till well after twelve, with the lights out and the window open.

VINNIE: It's after twelve. How much longer do we have to sit here?

BERYL: Shhh!

VINNIE: So what did Andy tell you? Are you going to let me in on the secret?

BERYL: No. I don't trust you.

VINNIE: If you can't trust your sister, you can't trust anyone.

BERYL: I *don't* trust anyone . . . Hah!

VINNIE: What?

BERYL: This is it!

SOUND OF BERYL SCRAMBLING OUT OF WINDOW.

VINNIE: Wait for me!

VINNIE/NARR: Beryl climbed out the window and I followed her. As we crept stealthily up to the chicken coop, I couldn't hear a thing. But, sneaking round the side of the shed, we came upon a strange sight. There, removing the screen from the chicken house window, was Uncle Donald, and there beside him, running his cigarette lighter up and down a long pole, was Clyde Fenstrom!

SQUAWKING! WOMEN SHOUTING, MEN LAUGHING AND GENERAL BALLYHOO.

BERYL: I'll murder you! No! Death's too good for you! Ohh!

CLYDE: Ouch! Take it easy!

SCENE FOURTEEN

VINNIE/NARR: The morning after she caught Clyde and Uncle Donald lifting her chickens Beryl was pale and subdued.

CUPS AND SAUCERS CLINKING AND OTHER BREAKFAST SOUNDS.

ANDY: Anyone want that piece of toast?

NELLIE: I still don't understand. What exactly were the boys doing last night?

BERYL: (MUTTERING.) Boys? Thieves!

ANDY: It's simple. If you put a heated pole next to a chicken on a cold night, they're bound to step on it, it's so nice and warm beneath their feet. They don't even wake up. You just pull them out the window.

BERYL: I don't want to talk about this, okay?

LEO: You should be happy you solved the mystery.

BERYL: Happy! While I was trying to stop those two . . .

ANDY: Murder them you mean. Clyde has a black eye.

BERYL: I wish it was *two* black eyes! I wish it was a broken neck!

BERYL STOMPS OUT.

LEO: Beryl, come back. Why's she so upset?

ANDY: While she was clobbering Clyde and Uncle Donald, another five chickens got away.

LEO: The real reason she's angry is that more didn't get away. There's still about seventy chickens between her and wedded bliss.

NELLIE: Not every woman sees getting a man as the be-all and end-all of life, Leo.

LEO: You certainly jumped when you saw your chance.

NELLIE: Jump! I've done nothing but jump since we met!

LEO: Well, you're always in the road!

FADE INTO "WHEN YOU WORE A TULIP"
SUNG RIOTOUSLY BY THE RANDALL FAMILY
ACCOMPANIED BY PIANO.

EPISODE THREE

RANDALL FAMILY SINGING "WHEN YOU WORE A TULIP."

SCENE ONE

THUNDERSTORM, RAIN.

LEO: Get that lantern in there. They must have a light.

BERYL: I can't get it lit.

LEO: Give it here. I'll do it. There.

BERYL: Oh God! Look at them all!

LEO: Now Beryl. You saved most of them. This'll keep them off each other's backs.

VINNIE/NARR: Beryl's troubles with her chickens were far from over. In early February there was a violent storm and thirty chickens smothered in the frantic crowding and scrambling that ensued. Clyde's sympathetic comments the next day did nothing to improve Beryl's frame of mind.

A week or two later, when a coyote got into the pen and another three were polished off, Clyde was even more solicitous.

SCENE TWO

CLUCKING AND FUSS.

BERYL: (MUTTERING.) Damn it. No! I don't believe it.

CLYDE: (APPROACHING.) Beryl? What's wrong. What on earth happened?

BERYL: As if you didn't know.

CLYDE: You want some help with this?

BERYL: Help? Get out of here you . . . you saboteur!

CLYDE: I hope I have better ideas in the area of sabotage than coyotes. Clean it up yourself!

VINNIE: After that, Clyde seemed to take no further interest in Beryl's chickens. There were other troubles in store, however, much more deadly and inevitable than Clyde.

In April Dad acquired his first tractor. A secondhand Massey 21 self-propelled.

SCENE THREE

TRACTOR SOUND FAINTLY IN BACKGROUND, FLUTTERING AND SQUAWKING.

BERYL: Mother! You've got to do something about Dad and that tractor. He's run over six chickens in three days!

MIXMASTER WHIRRING.

NELLIE: Well dear, shouldn't they be in the pen? Could you hand me those eggs?

BERYL: Someone keeps letting them out.

NELLIE: Surely not.

BERYL: They don't let themselves out.

TRACTOR SOUNDS GETTING GRADUALLY LOUDER.

BERYL: Look at him. He's a menace.

STIRRING BOWL WITH SPOON.

NELLIE: He'll be all right once he gets the hang of it. Reach me that cake pan, would you.

BERYL: Well, I hope he gets the hang of it before he does in all my chickens.

SCRAPING CONTENTS OF BOWL INTO PAN.

NELLIE: I'm sure he doesn't mean to, Beryl.

BERYL: Are you? *I* think he's doing it on purpose.

NELLIE: It's like when he runs me over. That's not on purpose.

BERYL: (UNDER HER BREATH.) Oh no?

NELLIE: I sometimes think your father's vision isn't all that good.

TRACTOR VERY LOUD.

BERYL: I'd stay out of his way for a while, if I were you. Don't even go outside when he's driving that thing. The opportunities for damage . . . What the . . . ? What's he backing up for? There isn't any room to back up.

NELLIE: Leo!

BERYL: He's going to hit the house! Mum! Jump!

CRASHING AND CRUNCHING ENGINE. THEN SUDDEN SILENCE EXCEPT FOR MAJOR HISSING SOUNDS.

LEO: Now how did *that* happen! Nellie! What are you doing here?

NELLIE: No Leo. What are *you* doing here? This is my kitchen. Mine!!!

SCENE FOUR

FAINT SOUND OF RANDALLS SINGING "WHEN YOU WORE A TULIP."

VINNIE/NARR: When I look back, I really wonder how it was we were all so darned happy. I guess maybe happiness and love were simpler then. You didn't have your expectations built up by the TV maybe? I mean, there was Mother who'd come within inches of being impaled by Dad's Massey 21 self-propelled . . .

BERYL: Not to mention the fact that all their savings for the past five years had to go into rebuilding the kitchen wall and repairing the tractor.

VINNIE/NARR: But even so, Mother was as happy as a newlywed.

BERYL: I guess she bought that old saw about the course of true love never running smooth.

SCENE FIVE

CHICKENS CLUCKING.

BERYL: Come on. Come on there. Come and get it.

CHICKENS CLUCKING AND FLAPPING.

VINNIE/NARR: It wasn't running all that smoothly for Beryl either. Not from the looks of her. The practical jokes were over. Uncle Donald was taking a course in Psychology, and Clyde, well who knew what he was up to. At any rate the chicken operation settled down and Beryl was all business again, caring for her little flock and studying her pamphlets. But occasionally you would come upon her gazing wistfully out of the window. If you said anything she quickly went back to her books.

LEO: And you know why, eh? She was winning the bet. She had two dozen healthy chickens on her hands, July was coming up fast and it was clear that Clyde wasn't going to bail her out.

NELLIE: Leo.

LEO: Just saying.

SCENE SIX

CHINKING OF DISHES.

VINNIE: Come on Andy. It's your turn to wash.

ANDY: I'll trade you

VINNIE: Okay. I'll wash. But you have to dry them *and* put them away.

DISHWASHING SOUNDS. ANDY WHISTLING.

ANDY: Wanna hear something interesting?

VINNIE: Is it gonna cost me?

ANDY: Clyde's got a girlfriend.

VINNIE: What? You're joking.

ANDY: No. It's Nora Tamprey. They go to the movies together, and dances and stuff.

VINNIE: Nora Tamprey? I don't believe it.

ANDY: It's true. I saw them together.

VINNIE: Well, keep it to yourself.

VINNIE/NARR: Nora Tamprey was considered a hot number by most of the young men in the district. She was disgustingly adorable, with silky brown curls and a pert way of looking limpidly up at whoever happened to be looking down at her. And she could cook too. We didn't see Clyde at all for some time after that. Then one day he turned up.

SCENE SEVEN

WOMEN'S VOICES. TEACUPS CLINKING. MEN ARRIVING. GREETINGS.

NELLIE: Hand me that platter, will you Vinnie.

BERYL: Has anyone seen the cream jug? I've got the sugar bowl, but I can't find the jug anywhere.

VINNIE: Mum, how many of these should I put out?

NELLIE: That's plenty, Dear.

VINNIE/NARR: It was near the end of July, two days in fact before Beryl's year was up. It was the day the Women's Institute met and it was our turn to have them. The meeting had proceeded as usual—nothing outstanding about it. Beryl, Mother, and I had retired to the kitchen, laying out cookies and slicing cakes. Everybody brought something for the tea that followed these meetings and, as the men would invariably turn up in time to join in before taking the wives home, it was always a good spread.

LEO: The guys are starting to arrive, Nellie.

NELLIE: Yes, Dear.

LEO: These Beryl's brownies?

NELLIE: Yes. They're exceptionally good.

LEO: (CHEWING.) Hmm hmm! Beryl's cooking goes a long way in making up for her looks.

NELLIE: Beryl has character. Some men like character.

LEO: Most men will take good cooking over character.

NELLIE: Oh, for pity's sake, Leo. Get out from underfoot!

SCENE EIGHT

VINNIE/NARR: Whatever they thought men liked, the women brought their best baking to the monthly meetings. Some were a little stingy, but it was still their best.

There was usually a rush for Nora Tamprey's butter nut-cake. She only ever brought one small loaf, but it was always the first thing to get eaten. Personally, I never thought her in Beryl's league as a cook, but brown curls and soulful looks can go a long way to teasing a palate.

Naomi Prince brought peas that day.

BERYL: Naomi Prince always brought peas. The poorest woman in the club would scrimp and scrape to bring her best but Naomi brought peas.

NELLIE: Now Beryl, be charitable.

BERYL: She'd come into the kitchen and bestow those wretched peas on you as though they were the treasure of the Pharaohs.

SCENE NINE

TEA PARTY. SPORADIC CHICKEN SOUNDS THROUGH WINDOW.

VINNIE/NARR: On the day I'm talking about, Naomi Prince came sidling in as usual, with the jar in her gloved hands.

NAOMI: A little something to stretch out the meal, Beryl. I never like to come empty-handed.

BERYL: Thanks, Naomi. What a treat.

NELLIE: (UNDER HER BREATH.) Beryl.

BERYL: Well, honestly. You'd think it was her last pot of caviar or something.

NELLIE: Shhh!

BERYL: She can't hear me. She's back in the parlour presiding over the company. Peas! At a tea party.

NELLIE: Open them up, and Vinnie, you butter some bread and make a little salad, so they won't look out of place.

VINNIE: Aw!

BERYL: (SNIFFS.) They've gone off.

NELLIE: Don't, Beryl. She means well.

BERYL: No, really. These peas are spoiled! We'll have them all dropping like flies if we put these out.

NELLIE: Oh dear! Well, just put out a jar of ours. She'll never know.

BERYL: Yes, she will. Ours aren't off.

NELLIE: Put them in the Delft bowl. Drain them first. And get rid of Naomi's peas, so she doesn't suspect.

VINNIE/NARR: Beryl obediently carried Naomi's jar to the window and tossed its contents into the yard

CHICKENS CLUCKING CONTENTEDLY.

SCENE TEN

TEAPARTY HUBBUB.

NAOMI: So, Leo, my dear. I heard you had a little incident with your new tractor. How is the tractor?

LEO: Oh, she's fine, Naomi.

NAOMI: I hear it was a close call for Eleanor.

LEO: It wasn't that close.

UNCLE DONALD: Came within an inch of pinning her to the ice box. We needed a block and tackle to get her out.

LEO: No need to exaggerate, Donald. (TRAILS OFF.) Guess I'll go see how the women are doing.

NAOMI: So how did you do in your Psychology course, Donald?

UNCLE DONALD: Passed with flying colours, Naomi.

NAOMI: Education can polish even the roughest diamond, Donald.

TEA PARTY SOUNDS, CLINKING CUPS AND CHATTER.

NELLIE: More tea anyone?

LEO: Have you tried these oatmeal squares, Nellie? You should see if you can get the recipe.

NELLIE: They're *my* oatmeal squares, Leo.

LEO: Oh. Well, um . . . great squares, honey!

SCENE ELEVEN

VINNIE/NARR: As usual, the get together was a great success. Everyone was into their third or fourth cup of tea when Clyde rode into the front yard. I could see him through the parlour window, and I could see Beryl watching him. The look on her face was reminiscent of the look she'd had sniffing Naomi's peas.

LEO: Beryl looks like she could wring a few necks.

UNCLE DONALD: Is that chicken necks?

SUPPRESSED LAUGHTER.

VINNIE/NARR: Beryl was showing the strain, I thought. She was definitely winning her bet with Clyde. With two dozen chickens free-grazing and healthy out in our yard she was home free. But looking at her looking out at Clyde and seeing the sickening way Nora Tamprey kept fending off Uncle Donald from "Clyde's piece" of her butter nut-cake, I wondered if she might be having second thoughts about independence.

BERYL: Now Donald, you'd better keep away from that cake. Nora's saving it for Clyde.

UNCLE DONALD: I don't think Clyde likes butter nut-cake all that much Beryl.

BERYL: He can't get enough of it, Donald. Trust me.

VINNIE/NARR: Clyde walked his horse round to the back to tether it and a few minutes later came in through the kitchen to the parlour. He made straight for Beryl, causing, I was pleased to see, a distinct ripple in Nora Tamprey's deportment. He flashed his buccaneer grin and clasped Beryl's hand gallantly. It was just like the movies.

CLYDE: Well, Beryl, I guess this is as good a time as any to announce our engagement.

TEA PARTY HUBBUB SUDDENLY ARRESTED.

LEO: Engagement? Did he say engagement?

ANDY: There's still two days to go with the bet, Clyde.

BERYL: And two dozen healthy chickens out back.

CLYDE: There are certainly two dozen. I counted them. But as to the state of their health . . . you'd have trouble convincing a dyed-in-the-wool optimist that they possess an ounce of health between them.

BERYL: What are you talking about?

CLYDE: See for yourself.

VINNIE/NARR: It was a strange moment, and one I've never forgotten, a moment suspended in time. Beryl's narrow-eyed glare seemed to take in the whole room, to spotlight it in some curious way. I was aware of every face present, of Dad impaled on the suspense of the moment, of Mother not suspenseful at all but beaming pleasantly. Of Nora whose ripple was turning into a tidal wave, of Donald cheerfully wolfing down the last piece of butter nut-cake.

BERYL: Those chickens are in perfect health.

CLYDE: In that case, they're giving the best imitation of playing dead I've ever seen.

VINNIE/NARR: Beryl looked at Clyde blankly for a moment, then leapt up and rushed out to the back yard. We followed her like a single animal.

RUSHING FEET AND MURMUR OF THE CROWD.

BERYL: If you've done anything to those chickens, Clyde Fenstrom!

EXCLAMATIONS OF DISBELIEF.

VINNIE/NARR: Everybody poured out into the yard and stopped dead in amazement. It was an unforgettable sight. There, flopped pathetically and mortally about the yard were Beryl's two dozen chickens and scattered here and there amongst the feathery corpses, gleaming innocently in the sunlight, were those criminal peas.

SCENE TWELVE

CAR. BIRDSONG. FAINT STRAINS OF "WHEN YOU WORE A TULIP."

VINNIE/NARR: The wedding took place in September on one of those beautiful post-harvest days where the stubble makes your eyes hurt it's so golden. We all went together in the same car, Beryl in the seat of honour in the front with Father, the rest of us crushed together in the back.

VINNIE: Beryl, you look terrific. Doesn't she look terrific?

NELLIE: The Lord does indeed move in mysterious ways, doesn't he?

LEO: (KNOWING LAUGH.) The Lord isn't the only one with mysterious tricks up his sleeve.

NELLIE: Really, Leo!

UNCLE DONALD: No, no. What it is, it's Freudian.

ANDY: What's Freudian?

LEO: You've been taking too many correspondence courses, Donald.

UNCLE DONALD: I'm serious. Beryl threw those peas out the window knowing in her unconscious mind that the chickens would eat them, an unthinking act on the surface but deliberately willed by something inside her that was out for her best interests.

ANDY: Huh?

LEO: That's a load of . . .

NELLIE: Leo!

LEO: What does Beryl have to say about it?

VINNIE/NARR: Beryl adjusted her veil and said nothing at all.

SCENE THIRTEEN

PIANO STARTS UP.

UNCLE DONALD: Yeah Beryl, you never did say much about those peas.

BERYL: Silence is golden, Uncle Donald.

LEO: Loose lips sink ships.

LOUD AND RIOTOUS THEY ALL LAUNCH INTO "WHEN YOU WORE A TULIP."

EPISODE FOUR

SCENE ONE

THE RANDALLS SINGING "WHEN YOU WORE A TULIP" AROUND THE PIANO CONTINUES UNDER NARRATION.

VINNIE/NARR: There is a general conviction among Easterners, at least among the Easterners that I've come across, that we in the west are a pretty simple bunch. Maybe they think because the depression honed us down to the basics of survival it honed us down emotionally and intellectually as well. I can't speak for the rest of the west but in Thigh Bone we're as advanced in the ways of intrigue and willfulness as any Easterner, perhaps more so. As proof of this you don't have to go any further than Hallie Bedford.

BERYL: Oh-oh, Uncle Donald. She's going to tell about Hallie.

UNCLE DONALD: Well, if you're going to talk about ornery women, you might as well talk about Hallie.

BERYL: Wooooh! Aren't we touchy?

UNCLE DONALD: In courtship Hallie was one mean little weasel.

BERYL: She wasn't the sneaky one.

UNCLE DONALD: She had her moments, but you're right. She didn't even come close to some people in sneakiness.

BERYL: Including yourself.

VINNIE/NARR: Well, I won't say who was the sneakiest, but the entanglements and double-crosses that went on in the wooing and claiming of Hallie Bedford made Machiavelli seem like a grade schooler.

SCENE TWO

DISTANT TRAIN WHISTLE AND APPROACH OF TRAIN.

VINNIE/NARR: When Hallie came to teach at Thigh Bone School in the fall of 1949, she was the fifth new teacher in five years. Her predecessors had all been good looking, female and unmarried. They were all engaged to be married by the end of their first month on the job. They had all married men from the same family—Charlie, Arthur, Jim, and Hugh Lang. There was only one Lang brother left—Parnell. When Hallie Bedford stepped down from the train at the Thigh Bone Station that fine September morning it was the unshakable belief of almost everyone in the area that she and Parnell Lang were a foregone conclusion.

TRAIN WHISTLE AND APPROACH OF TRAIN CLOSER NOW. HUM OF BYSTANDERS.

PARNELL: Only an hour late, Donald.

UNCLE DONALD: You could practically say she's on time, Parnell.

ARRIVAL OF TRAIN, BURST OF STEAM.

VINNIE/NARR: Uncle Donald and I were among the inquisitive crowd who gathered to witness Hallie's arrival. Donald was a drinking buddy of Parnell's, so we were fortunate enough to be with the incumbent groom when the train finally arrived and its single passenger for Thigh Bone dismounted.

SCENE THREE

CONDUCTOR: (FROM A DISTANCE.) Watch your step, Miss.

HALLIE: I'm all right, thank you. You could help me with my luggage, though, if you wouldn't mind.

CONDUCTOR: Sure thing.

HALLIE: Both those big cases. And that big box.

VINNIE/NARR: I was really impressed with Hallie. She seemed to me modern woman personified. Smartly dressed, beautiful in a handsome rather than a pretty way, there was an air of confidence about her. Her manner, as she ordered her luggage off the train, was crisp and pleasant.

CONDUCTOR: There you go.

HALLIE: Careful! That's very fragile.

CONDUCTOR: Not to worry.

UNCLE DONALD: So. What do you think, Parnell?

PARNELL: A little on the bossy side, eh?

UNCLE DONALD: She's spirited, Parnell. A woman of character.

PARNELL: Think I'll wait for the next one.

UNCLE DONALD: You might be waiting a while. This one looks like she might settle in. She might stay on the job for years.

PARNELL: Maybe I was meant to be one of life's bachelors.

VINNIE: Too bad. She seems nice, Parnell.

UNCLE DONALD: She probably has money too.

PARNELL: You think so? Hmm . . . Nah! It ain't worth giving up my independence. Besides, she's twenty-eight years old, eh? That's what Jeff Boggs told me. He's the one handled her application. Twenty-eight's pretty old.

UNCLE DONALD: You're thirty-two, Parnell!

PARNELL: Yeah. But it's different for a guy, eh? (MOVES OFF.) See ya Donald. Vinnie.

FEET MOVING OFF ALONG STATION'S WOODEN PLATFORM.

UNCLE DONALD: Yeah. So long, Parnell.

VINNIE: So, do you think he'll pop the question?

UNCLE DONALD: When he knows he's doomed from the start? Parnell doesn't need a wife, he needs a keeper. A woman like that would never have him and he knows it.

VINNIE: You're probably right.

UNCLE DONALD: Of course I'm right. A woman like that, she would be looking for something more stimulating in a partnership than Parnell would have to offer. A woman like that . . .

VINNIE: Do I detect a note of interest in her yourself, Uncle Donald?

UNCLE DONALD: Certainly not. You know I can't afford to be interested in anyone right now. I have my future to think about, Vinnie.

VINNIE: Of course. Your future.

UNCLE DONALD: Don't be disrespectful, Vinnie. It doesn't become you.

VINNIE/NARR: Uncle Donald's future was an ongoing item in the annals of our family life. For as far back as I could remember it was Donald's dream to go to university and become a lawyer. But one thing or another, not to mention the Second World War, kept getting in the way. He had been saving every penny he earned, taking correspondence courses in the meantime. His goal was three years of university by correspondence and three thousand dollars in the bank to attend law school. By the fall of 1949 he'd completed two years and saved over a thousand dollars.

UNCLE DONALD: No, Vinnie. Marriage and family life are not in my immediate future, I'm afraid. And they're certainly not in Parnell's either.

SCENE FOUR

VINNIE/NARR: Uncle Donald was undoubtedly sincere in saying this to me, but he was shortly to make a complete about face on his opinion about Parnell and Hallie. We were over at Clyde and Beryl's for a game of cards.

SHUFFLING CARDS AND RADIO IN BACKGROUND

UNCLE DONALD: Your deal, Clyde.

BERYL: Send the popcorn this way, would you. I'm famished. Thanks.

CRUNCHING POPCORN.

VINNIE: Clyde! What kind of a hand is this?

CLYDE: A losing hand, I hope. Donald and I mean to mop up.

VINNIE: Pass!

UNCLE DONALD: Pick it up, Clyde.

CLYDE: Play it, Uncle!

VINNIE/NARR: After their marriage Beryl and Clyde had managed to scrape together the down payment on a quarter section and Beryl had begun chicken farming in earnest. With Clyde's job at the elevator and her small earnings they were making a go of it, but just barely. Their house was primitive, two granaries shoved together in an L-shape, but it was cheerful and lively. Uncle Donald often drove me over there for popcorn and a game of euchre.

CLYDE: So, what's the new teacher like?

VINNIE: I think Uncle Donald's sweet on her.

UNCLE DONALD: I merely said she wasn't the type to be attracted to Parnell Lang.

BERYL: Why not?

UNCLE DONALD: Well. You know what Parnell's like.

BERYL: Yeah. He's dishy.

CLYDE: Parnell Lang? He's a sleaze and a loafer.

BERYL: I didn't say nice, I said dishy. Compelling in a louche kind of way. You know what I mean.

CLYDE: No. I don't.

VINNIE: Is anyone going to *do* anything?

UNCLE DONALD: Yeah. Ace takes your King.

VINNIE: Rats!

SLAMMING DOWN OF BERYL'S CARD.
DONALD'S GROAN.

BERYL: Trumped ya. Parnell's the kind of man women ruin themselves over.

CLYDE: That's nonsense! Your lead.

UNCLE DONALD: Well, you can take my word for it. There may be women who would ruin themselves over the likes of Parnell Lang but Hallie Bedford isn't one of them. Left bower takes it.

BERYL: You're in the minority, Uncle Donald. Everyone I've talked to is betting that Hallie and Parnell will tie the knot.

UNCLE DONALD: Really? I'm sorely tempted to meet those bets. Gambling on the unreasoning romanticism of your average prairie dweller. There's money to be made.

CLYDE: Someone's beaten you to it.

BERYL: Who?

CLYDE: Nora Tamprey. She's giving two-to-one odds to anyone who says the marriage will take place.

UNCLE DONALD: She's going to clean up.

BERYL: How do you know what Nora Tamprey's up to?

CLYDE: She'd like to clean up. But so far she's only taken in about $250.00. She was hoping for a romantic with a lot of money.

BERYL: Clyde! I said, how do you know what Nora Tamprey's up to?

CLYDE: She was at the café at lunch time today.

BERYL: You were having lunch with her?

VINNIE: It's your deal, Beryl.

BERYL: I want to know about this lunch date with Nora.

CLYDE: It wasn't a date. She was just there. She was looking for suckers with money to lose.

UNCLE DONALD: How much money? Did she say?

CLYDE: I got the impression she'd take on as much as a thousand dollars.

UNCLE DONALD: She can give two-to-one odds on a thousand?

CLYDE: She's got about four thousand in the bank. But as you say, she's not taking any risks. It's not likely they will get married.

BERYL: How do you know she has four thousand in the bank?

UNCLE DONALD: Two-to-one, eh? I could double my money and . . .

CLYDE: (CAUTIONARY.) Donald? What are you up to?

VINNIE: It's your turn, Beryl.

BERYL: Pass. I don't like this at all.

CLYDE: Don't worry. Donald wouldn't bet a thousand bucks against a sure thing. Pass . . . would you?

VINNIE: Pass.

UNCLE DONALD: Make it hearts.

BERYL: Nora would never accept such a big bet.

CLYDE: She'd be a fool not to.

VINNIE: What big bet are we talking about?

CLYDE: Donald's going to bet his college money with Nora.

VINNIE: On Parnell and Hallie? The whole thousand?

BERYL: Speaking of Nora. You still haven't explained about lunch.

VINNIE/NARR: Donald didn't say anything more that evening, but it was obvious to all of us that he had made up his mind to bet the wad that Parnell would ask Hallie to marry him, and that Hallie would accept. Even though minutes before he had said there wasn't a chance in the world that this would ever happen.

But here in the west, Love does crazy things to people, and not only to lovers. The onlookers are in just as much danger of getting caught up in the battle. Uncle Donald was about to embark on a venture fraught with risk and peril.

The first thing he did was get himself over to the school and scout the territory.

SCENE FIVE

CHILDREN: Red Rover, Red Rover, let Charlie come over!

SCREAMS AND SHOUTS AND PILEUP OF CHILDREN.

UNCLE DONALD: Hi there.

HALLIE: Hello.

UNCLE DONALD: I'm Donald Ross. I popped over to see if there was anything you needed.

HALLIE: There is. I'm not sure how to work the heater.

UNCLE DONALD: Jeff Boggs will probably know. I'll check it out for you.

HALLIE: If it's not too much trouble.

UNCLE DONALD: None at all.

HALLIE: I thought I should learn how before the cold weather starts.

UNCLE DONALD: Good idea.

AWKWARD MOMENT OF SILENCE.

HALLIE: Does it get very cold here?

UNCLE DONALD: Does it get cold. Listen. If you throw a bucket of water in the air, it freezes before it hits the ground.

HALLIE: (LAUGHS.) I'd better master that heater then. Um. I should ring the bell. It was lovely meeting you, Mr. Ross.

UNCLE DONALD: Donald, please. There are lots of others just like me, you know. Come to the dance Saturday if you want to meet them.

HALLIE: Dance? Where would that be?

UNCLE DONALD: Right here. In the school. (BOTH LAUGH.)

BELL RINGING! CHILDREN YELLING!

SCENE SIX

TINKERING WITH TRACTOR.

LEO: You mean Nora Tamprey actually took Donald's bet. Hand me that wrench, would you.

BERYL: If they get engaged before Christmas, Donald makes two thousand bucks. Try tightening that nut there.

LEO: Don't get in my way, Beryl. It's hard to say who's the bigger fool, Donald or Nora. I mean a bet's one thing. This is major gambling!

CLUNKING SOUND.

LEO: I dunno. I'm going to have to get Billy Coulter to take a look at this. I don't know what the heck I'm doing.

BERYL: It's never been the same since you backed it into Mother.

LEO: I did not back it into your mother. I backed it into the house.

BERYL: Same thing. Can I have a go before you phone?

LEO: You can *not*! I've put enough money into this pile of tin.

BERYL: Just let me try one thing, Dad

LEO: No! I'm going to phone Billy right now. (FADING OFF.) Maybe he can look at it today.

FOOTSTEPS CRUCHING OFF.
BERYL HUMS AND TINKERS FOR A MOMENT.
TRACTOR STARTS UP.

BERYL: YES!

LEO: (FROM AFAR.) I told you not to touch that.

BERYL: I got it working, didn't I?

LEO: (FROM AFAR.) Turn that thing off!

BERYL: Okay. You don't have to get snorty.

TURNS TRACTOR OFF.

SCENE SEVEN

VINNIE/NARR: One thing that was clear about Hallie from the very beginning was that she was super independent. The school committee had room and board all set up for her when she arrived, but she wasn't having any of it

HALLIE: I don't want to hurt any feelings, Mr. Boggs, but I really must have my own place.

BOGGS: You want to build a house, you mean?

HALLIE: There must be something in town I can rent.

BOGGS: There's a couple of places on the other side of the river. But nothing in town.

HALLIE: What about that grocery store on Front Street. It has an upstairs and I don't see any sign of occupancy.

BOGGS: No one's living in it. I believe it's filled with supplies and stuff.

SCENE EIGHT

TOWN. STREET. PEOPLE AND CARS.

NELLIE: That new teacher's moved in over Jenson's store.

LEO: What does she want to live there for?

NELLIE: Likes her independence, I guess.

LEO: Too darned independent if you ask me.

NELLIE: There no such thing as too independent.

LEO: You want Donald to lose his money.

NELLIE: As far as I can see he's already lost it.

SCENE NINE

VINNIE/NARR: It was clear that confronted with the possibility of tripling his savings, Donald had flown in the face of his own reason. He was counting on the dance at the school as a means of getting the prospective lovers together. On Saturday he drove all the way to Calgary to buy flowers, and duly turned up with them at Parnell's place.

PARNELL: Flowers. F'me?

UNCLE DONALD: Dammit, Parnell! You've been drinking. You can't go to the dance like this.

PARNELL: Why not?

UNCLE DONALD: Oh heck!

SCENE TEN

VINNIE/NARR: Uncle Donald set to work. Getting Parnell ready for the dance was no small operation He had to iron his shirt. Make him coffee. Sober him up. By the time they got to the dance the card games were long over and the dancers had all paired off. As for Hallie Bedford, she had joined up with the young teacher from the next school district.

RADIO MUSIC. DANCE SOUNDS. HUBBUB.

HALLIE: Hello, Mr. Ross.

UNCLE DONALD: Oh. Donald, please. Miss Bedford, there's someone I'd like you to meet. He's right over there.

HALLIE: You mean Parnell. I've heard the predictions. Ridiculous, isn't it? As if I could even think of marrying someone like that.

UNCLE DONALD: Oh? But Parnell is salt of the earth.

HALLIE: Really?

UNCLE DONALD: Parnell is the epitome of the western man. He's one of that breed who arrive here with ten dollars in their pockets and high hopes.

HALLIE: I understood he was born here.

UNCLE DONALD: Uh, he was. I was speaking figuratively.

HALLIE: I see. Well in my books, Mr. Lang is one of those people who should be advised to wear a hat when he's riding a donkey.

UNCLE DONALD: Why is that?

HALLIE: So it's clear which one is which.

SCENE ELEVEN

BACKGROUND PIANO.

LEO: That Hallie. She had a lip on her didn't she?

UNCLE DONALD: Still does.

BERYL: Yep. She still does

LAUGHTER. ALL SINGING “WHEN YOU WORE A TULIP.”

EPISODE FIVE

SCENE ONE

"WHEN YOU WORE A TULIP" SUNG BY THE RANDALL FAMILY, GATHERED AROUND THE PIANO. THE SONG FADES INTO THE NARRATION.

VINNIE/NARR: All that fall and well into the winter Uncle Donald continued his mission to bring Parnell Lang and Hallie Bedford to the altar. We still refer to this time as Donald's mad period.

LEO: Well now, Donald always liked a good joke.

UNCLE DONALD: Depending on who the joke's on.

BERYL: You just made a bad judgement.

UNCLE DONALD: You're the one who said Parnell was dishy. I thought Hallie would think so too.

VINNIE/NARR: Madness or bad judgement, Donald convinced himself that Hallie could be made to marry Parnell.

One of the ways he meant to bring this about was to make Parnell seem a more attractive catch. Parnell was good looking in a sinister kind of way and Donald had the idea he could be enhanced. He persuaded Parnell to get a haircut. He personally had all Parnell's clothes cleaned and laundered and tried to persuade him to give up his more unappealing habits, like chewing tobacco. Over the space of a month he worked quite a transformation on Parnell. And it was having the desired effect with every single woman in the area except Hallie Bedford.

SCENE TWO

COFFEE CUPS AND KITCHEN RADIO.

LEO: It's like ants to honey. I never see that fellow Parnell without there being three or four women clinging to him.

BERYL: Just not the one Donald's hoping will cling to him.

LEO: Where is Donald, anyway? He's never around anymore.

BERYL: He's over at Parnell's. Fixing up his house. In the last six weeks he's put in plumbing and painted the place top to bottom.

LEO: He's crazy!

BERYL: Round the bend.

LEO: Your mother's real worried about him.

BERYL: With good reason.

SCENE THREE

VINNIE/NARR: Donald did seem to be working at preserving his investment beyond all reason. He was also bringing his powers of persuasion to bear on Hallie. He appeared at the school on a regular basis to keep the heater running but would end up spending long hours in conversation. His initial topic was always Parnell, but Hallie would deftly turn the conversation to other topics.

TINKERING WITH HEATER.

HALLIE: Tell me more about your sister.

UNCLE DONALD: There's not much more I can tell you. Nellie's one of those people destined to be happy no matter what.

HALLIE: I can't believe she puts up with Leo the way she does. Has he run her over lately?

UNCLE DONALD: There was a dangerous incident the other week with the new power mower, but Nell managed to scramble onto the porch in time.

HALLIE: He never lets up, does he!

UNCLE DONALD: Well Sis is nimble, you know. She manages to stay out of harm's way. There, that should be okay for a while.

HALLIE: Thanks, Donald. I've made some coffee. Would you like some?

UNCLE DONALD: Sure would. Hey, what's this you're reading? Ogden Nash! I loved this book. "Candy's dandy."

HALLIE: "But liquor's quicker." (THEY BOTH LAUGH.) Well, you're going to have to make do with coffee.

UNCLE DONALD: Coffee's swell.

SCENE FOUR

TAVERN HUBBUB.

UNCLE DONALD: I don't see why you can't drop round and pass the time of day with her, Parnell.

PARNELL: I wouldn't know what to say to her, Donald.

UNCLE DONALD: Say what you say to all those other women you hang about with.

PARNELL: Are you kidding? She'd have me arrested!

UNCLE DONALD: Look, Parnell, will you at least give it a try?

PARNELL: I dunno. I need another drink, eh.

UNCLE DONALD: Oh, go ahead.

PARNELL: (MOVING OFF.) I'll just see if I can round up that barmaid.

TAVERN SOUNDS AND MUSIC.

NORA: Hi, Donald.

UNCLE DONALD: Nora. How are you doing?

NORA: Hear you've been working hard.

UNCLE DONALD: Well, I have been pretty . . .

NORA: Parnell showed me his place. You did a real nice job on it. You have a gift.

UNCLE DONALD: Well, thank you, Nora.

NORA: It won't be enough, though.

UNCLE DONALD: What do you mean?

NORA: Parnell has other fish to fry.

UNCLE DONALD: I know he likes to play the field. But he's ready to settle down, believe me.

PARNELL: Hi Nora! How about a drink.

NORA: Not this time, Parnell.

SCENE FIVE

VINNIE/NARR: Things came to a head on Hallowe'en night. It was your usual Hallowe'en. Trick-or-treating little goblins with their paper sacks. Teenage high jinks. Outhouses overturned, hopefully with the occupants inside. Windows soaped. Toilet paper flung about.

LAUGHTER. RUNNING. CRIES OF "TRICK OR TREAT!"

VINNIE/NARR: The moon was full that night, furry around the edges with a frost ring. It was the custom in those days for the kids to carry lanterns. Those oil lanterns. "Railway lanterns" we called them. You know the kind. Everyone had one or two kicking around.

RUNNING AND SHOUTING. CRIES OF "FIRE!"

SCENE SIX

PHONE RINGING AND BEING PICKED UP.

UNCLE DONALD: Hello?

BOGGS: Donald. Phil Boggs here. Thought I'd let you know. Not that there's much to be done. The Brigade did their best . . .

UNCLE DONALD: A fire?

BOGGS: Yeah. Some little goblins got careless and tipped a lantern over in the alley.

UNCLE DONALD: Where?

BOGGS: Jamieson's store.

UNCLE DONALD: Oh my God, Hallie!

PHONE DROPPING. DONALD EXITING.

BOGGS: She's okay. She got out right away. Donald? Donald!

TOWN HALL. COFFEE BEING POURED. MUCH TALK. FEET CLONKING ABOUT.

UNCLE DONALD: Hallie! Where is she?

BOGGS: Donald. Would you like a coffee?

UNCLE DONALD: What? No! Where's Hallie? . . .

BOGGS: I told you, she's fine.

UNCLE DONALD: I've got to find her! Hallie! Thank God you're all right! I've been beside myself.

HALLIE: (IRRITABLY.) Of course, I'm all right.

UNCLE DONALD: I don't know what I would have done, Hallie, if . . . Are you sure you're okay? You look terrible!

HALLIE: Thanks, Donald. I lost my hairbrush in the fire.

UNCLE DONALD: Hallie! That's not what I meant. I don't care if you look terrible as in appearance terrible. I'd love you even if you were terrible that way. I meant you look terrible as in awful and I . . .

HALLIE: Oh, shut up.

UNCLE DONALD: I want to marry you.

HALLIE: This is hardly the time . . .

UNCLE DONALD: No. I mean it! Marry me!

HALLIE: Donald, I really am not feeling my best, right now . . .

UNCLE DONALD: I want to marry you. I don't care if it's not the right time. Or that you're not feeling your best. I don't care about any of that. I don't even care about the money.

HALLIE: What money?

UNCLE DONALD: Uh. What. Money. Yes. Well.

VINNIE/NARR: It seems hard to believe, but somehow Hallie had missed hearing about Donald's bet. She knew people had mentally hitched her to Parnell but about the bets, about Nora and Donald's wager, she had not been informed.

Donald was to say later that he didn't know if it was his final act of madness or his first act of sanity. In any case, he confessed all.

UNCLE DONALD: So, you see, I, um, bet a thousand dollars that you and Parnell would get married by Christmas.

HALLIE: This is unbelievable! . . . I mean . . . You really thought I would marry Parnell!

UNCLE DONALD: Beryl told me he was attractive to women.

HALLIE: About as attractive as *flypaper.*

UNCLE DONALD: It seemed like a good idea at the time. I didn't know I was going to fall for you myself.

HALLIE: Don't touch me! You know, next to you, Parnell looks good. At least he's honest. At least he's not a lying . . . despicable . . .

UNCLE DONALD: Hallie, if you'd let me explain . . .

HALLIE: Don't talk to me . . . Ugh!! My grandmother was right!

UNCLE DONALD: What about?

HALLIE: She said, "Never look under a granary if you think there's a skunk."

VINNIE/NARR: And that was the last word Hallie had to say on the subject. Uncle Donald was desolate, but he hadn't yet been plunged to the depths of desolation. That came a few days later.

SCENE SEVEN

STREET SOUNDS.

PARNELL: Hi ya, Donald, old buddy.

UNCLE DONALD: Parnell.

PARNELL: You'd've been proud of me, Donny Boy. I finally popped the question.

UNCLE DONALD: You what? You asked her? What did she say?

PARNELL: She said yes! She said . . .

UNCLE DONALD: Oh God! I don't want to hear it.

PARNELL: Hey. I thought you'd be happy, eh?

UNCLE DONALD: I am. It's just that I'm not . . . yeah . . . I guess I'm not happy.

SCENE EIGHT

MEAL SOUNDS.

LEO: Isn't Donald eating with us.

VINNIE: He doesn't feel like it right now, Dad.

LEO: What's he so upset about? He doubled his money, didn't he.

VINNIE: I'll bet Nora's feeling a little blue today.

LEO: You know, that's something Donald should think about. He could do a lot worse than hitch up with Nora Tamprey. She's pretty, a good cook, rich. What more could he want?

VINNIE: He wants Hallie.

LEO: He does? . . . Then why did he . . .

DOOR OPENING.

BERYL: Here's Clyde.

LEO: Pull up a chair Clyde.

CLYDE: Hi folks. Hi Honey. You heard the bad news. (GENERAL RESPONSE.) How's he taking it?

BERYL: Not well.

CLYDE: I'd feel the same way. Losing all that money. I'd shoot myself.

VINNIE: He's not losing the money, Clyde. Parnell popped the question.

CLYDE: Well yeah. But not to Hallie.

VINNIE: What do you mean?

CLYDE: I thought you knew. Parnell's marrying Nora.

ALL: Nora!!! Donald! Donnie! Uncle Donald!

BERYL: That sidewinder! That snake!

LEO: I always said Nora Tamprey couldn't be trusted.

SCENE NINE

WEDDING MUSIC.

VINNIE/NARR: Nora and Parnell were married in the new year. It was a real bang-up wedding with a big reception in Drumheller. And it was a good marriage. With Nora's money they bought the Creely Hotel in Coal Hill and made a roaring success of it. There was a general outcry from those who lost bets to her, that she wasn't playing fair. That she had insider knowledge. Nora kept all the money without so much as a blush. Her attitude was that suckers and their money are soon parted.

SCENE TEN

VINNIE/NARR: Hallie eventually forgave Uncle Donald but not before she made him suffer for a while. She finally said yes to him just before school let out, and they were married that August.

It was pouring cats and dogs that day. Dad, Mum, Andy, and I went off together crammed into the Overland. We were wearing our Sunday best but feeling a little droopy from the damp. It was raining so hard we could scarcely see the road ahead. And the canvas roof canopy was less than waterproof.

RAIN. CAR INTERIOR.

LEO: It's coming down like the wrath of hell.

NELLIE: I don't know how you can see anything in this downpour. You should pull over till it lets up.

LEO: And miss the wedding? Sit back and stop worrying. I'm in control . . . Say!

BRAKING CAR.

ANDY: What?

LEO: A brand new sack of feed in the ditch. Must've fallen off some truck.

ANDY: I didn't see anything.

LEO: It's back there about a hundred feet. Just run back and get it, Nellie.

NELLIE: Yes, Dear.

CAR DOOR OPENING.

VINNIE/NARR: From sheer force of habit, mother got out in the downpour and ran back to the sack. It then occurred to Dad that he wasn't being a gentleman.

LEO: I'll just back up the car so she won't have to carry it so far.

CAR BACKING UP.

LEO: There's the feed sack, but where's your mother?

VINNIE: She's disappeared.

ANDY: Mum?

LEO: Damned if I know where she's got to.

VINNIE/NARR: Mother was nowhere to be seen. She'd totally disappeared. Then we looked out the front and there she was—flattened into the mud. Dad had backed right over her.

LEO: What the hell is she doing up there?

VINNIE/NARR: Mother rose up out of the mud like some avenging creature from Weird Tales and marched grimly back to the feed sack. She hurled it into the trunk, came round to the driver's side and opened the door.

CAR DOOR OPENING.

LEO: Lucky you weren't hurt, Nellie.

NELLIE: Move over.

LEO: What for?

NELLIE: (THROUGH HER TEETH.) Shove! Over!

SHOVING AND MOVING SOUNDS.

LEO: But Nellie!

NELLIE: I should have done this years ago. It just never occurred to me.

LEO: But you don't know how to drive, Nellie.

NELLIE: I'm going to learn, starting now. I'm driving back to the house to change. Then I'm driving us to the wedding.

CAR STARTING UP. GEARS CRUNCHING.

LEO: You're crunching the gears, Nellie!

NELLIE: I'll get the hang of it. Just give me time.

VINNIE: You're doing fine, Mum.

ANDY: (UNDER HIS BREATH.) You've got to be joking.

VINNIE/NARR: With Mother at the wheel, we moved smartly along in the old Overland.

ANDY: You're moving a little fast, Mum

NELLIE: Nonsense. Much easier to stay on the road if you keep to a certain speed. 'Specially in this mud.

LEO: There's lights up ahead.

NELLIE: I don't know why I didn't do this years ago. This is so much fun.

LEO: They're coming towards us, Nellie.

ANDY: Keep right, Mother!

LEO: Nellie!

OTHERS: Mum!

VEHICLES SCREECHING AND PASSING WAY TOO CLOSE.

LEO: You nearly hit that truck!

ANDY: Near miss, Mum.

NELLIE: Yes. Weren't we lucky!

VINNIE: Father didn't say anything, but from the look on his face it was obvious that his long-held notion of luck had changed direction about 180 degrees.

SCENE ELEVEN

PIANO PLAYING "WHEN YOU WORE A TULIP."

LEO: I'm getting tired of this song.

BERYL: Just one more chorus, Dad.

HALLIE: (ENTERING.) Hi everyone.

SEVERAL: Hallie!

BERYL: We've just been talking about you, Hallie. About you and Uncle Donald getting hitched and . . .

UNCLE DONALD: And all your tricky little ways.

HALLIE: You deserved everything you got.

UNCLE DONALD: Well, I know I got everything I deserved.

LEO: Quit your billing and cooing and let's get on with it.

"WHEN YOU WORE A TULIP" SUNG BY THE WHOLE RAUCOUS BUNCH SWELLS AND FADES SLOWLY OUT!

THE END

ACKNOWLEDGEMENTS

I will be eternally grateful to Martie Fishman, and the late Bill Lane and Mark Schoenberg, who welcomed me into the radio community and always encouraged the offbeat and unconventional—no matter how outrageous. And a special thank-you to all those impassioned actors, sound technicians, musicians, and production assistants, forever at the ready to lift a script off the page and bring it to exhilarating life.

I am also extremely indebted to the Brave & Brilliant team at the University of Calgary Press: series editor and my editor Aritha van Herk, director Brian Scrivener, designer Melina Cusano, editorial coordinator Helen Hajnoczky, marketing specialist Alison Cobra, and copy editor Andrew Goodwin, for their creative contributions and for giving these radio dramas a permanent home.

And special blessings to David and the boys, Michael, Luke, James and Colin, who supplied—in fact insisted on—the wild and nutty context in which these plays were conceived and written.

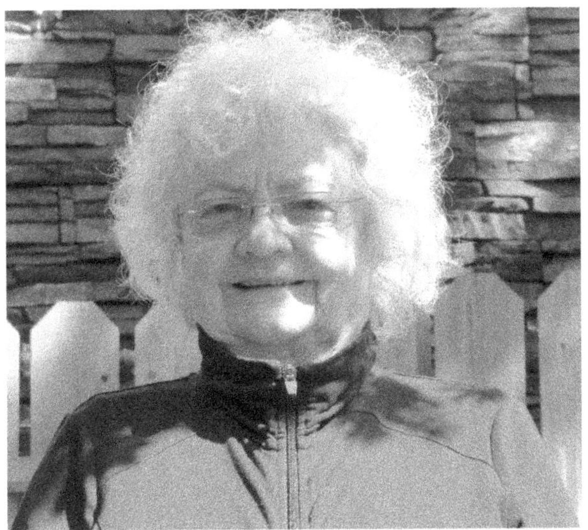

Photo Credit: David Scollard

Rose Scollard is an award-winning Calgary playwright who loves to explore themes from unexpected perspectives. She is the co-founder of Maenad Productions, Western Canada's first woman-centered theatre and author of *Tango Noir.* Together with her husband David, she also created the Calgary literary press Frontenac House.

 **BRAVE & BRILLIANT SERIES**

SERIES EDITOR: Aritha van Herk, Professor, English, University of Calgary
ISSN 2371-7238 (PRINT) ISSN 2371-7246 (ONLINE)

No. 1 · *The Book of Sensations* | Sheri-D Wilson
No. 2 · *Throwing the Diamond Hitch* | Emily Ursuliak
No. 3 · *Fail Safe* | Nikki Sheppy
No. 4 · *Quarry* | Tanis Franco
No. 5 · *Visible Cities* | Kathleen Wall and Veronica Geminder
No. 6 · *The Comedian* | Clem Martini
No. 7 · *The High Line Scavenger Hunt* | Lucas Crawford
No. 8 · *Exhibit* | Paul Zits
No. 9 · *Pugg's Portmanteau* | D. M. Bryan
No. 10 · *Dendrite Balconies* | Sean Braune
No. 11 · *The Red Chesterfield* | Wayne Arthurson
No. 12 · *Air Salt* | Ian Kinney
No. 13 · *Legislating Love* | Play by Natalie Meisner, with Director's Notes by Jason Mehmel, and Essays by Kevin Allen and Tereasa Maillie
No. 14 · *The Manhattan Project* | Ken Hunt
No. 15 · *Long Division* | Gil McElroy
No. 16 · *Disappearing in Reverse* | Allie McFarland
No. 17 · *Phillis* | Alison Clarke
No. 18 · *DR SAD* | David Bateman
No. 19 · *Unlocking* | Amy LeBlanc
No. 20 · *Spectral Living* | Andrea King
No. 21 · *Happy Sands* | Barb Howard
No. 22 · *In Singing, He Composed a Song* | Jeremy Stewart
No. 23 · *I Wish I Could be Peter Falk* | Paul Zits
No. 24 · *A Kid Called Chatter* | Chris Kelly
No. 25 · *the book of smaller* | rob mclennan
No. 26 · *An Orchid Astronomy* | Tasnuva Hayden
No. 27 · *Not the Apocalypse I Was Hoping For* | Leslie Greentree
No. 28 · *Refugia* | Patrick Horner
No. 29 · *Five Stalks of Grain* | Adrian Lysenko, Illustrated by Ivanka Theodosia Galadza
No. 30 · *body works* | dennis cooley
No. 31 · *East Grand Lake* | Tim Ryan
No. 32 · *Muster Points* | Lucas Crawford
No. 33 · *Flicker* | Lori Hahnel
No. 34 · *Flight Risk* | A Play by Meg Braem, with Essays by William John Pratt and by David B. Hogan and Philip D. St. John, and Director's Notes by Samantha MacDonald
No. 35 · *The Signs of No* | Judith Pond
No. 36 · *Limited Verse* | David Martin
No. 37 · *We Are Already Ghosts* | Kit Dobson
No. 38 · *Invisible Lives* | Cristalle Smith
No. 39 · *Recombinant Theory* | Joel Katelnikoff
No. 40 · *The Loom* | Andy Weaver
No. 41 · *Bonememory* | Anna Veprinska
No. 42 · *Love and War Western Style* | Rose Scollard

www.ingramcontent.com/pod-product-compliance
Lightning Source LLC
Chambersburg PA
CBHW041753010726
47507CB00009B/380

* 9 7 8 1 7 7 3 8 5 6 1 5 5 *